THE
WILLIAM POWELL
AND
MYRNA LOY
MURDER CASE

THE
WILLIAM POWELL
AND
MYRNA LOY
MURDER CASE

George Baxt

ST. MARTIN'S PRESS
NEW YORK

Production Editor: David Stanford Burr

Design: Nancy Resnick

Library of Congress Cataloging-in-Publication Data

Baxt, George.
    The William Powell and Myrna Loy murder case / by George Baxt.—1st ed.
        p.   cm.
    ISBN 0-312-14071-1
    1. Motion picture actors and actresses—California—Los Angeles—Fiction.   2. Hollywood (Los Angeles, Calif.)—Fiction.   3. Powell, William, 1892–1984—Fiction.   4. Loy, Myrna, 1905–1993—Fiction.
I. Title.
PS3552.A8478W55   1996
813'.54—dc20   95-33657
                                         CIP

First Edition: February 1996

10 9 8 7 6 5 4 3 2 1

For Kelley Ragland and Linda Parisi

THE
WILLIAM POWELL
AND
MYRNA LOY
MURDER CASE

O N E

$\mathcal{I}$t was December third, nineteen hundred and thirty-six, there were twenty-one shopping days until Christmas, and Myrna Loy wished she was in Timbuktu. Not because she was particularly interested in visiting the place, but the name sounded mysterious and exotic and at this moment Myrna (Minnie to her friends) wished she was anywhere but Los Angeles, and Timbuktu would do just fine. It was one of those damned hot days in Los Angeles when a swimming pool and a highball would be preferable to standing on a street corner wearing a suffocating chinchilla coat (not hers, but on loan to Metro-Goldwyn-Mayer, her employers).

"Asta! Stop being such a pest!" She had a tight grip on the dog's leash, the dog being very restless and, like Myrna, wondering when the photographer would settle on an angle that satisfied him. Myrna saw no reason to disguise her impatience. "Albert, for crying out loud do something!" Asta was straining to join Albert, who was fussing with the camera. "Asta, I'm losing my patience!" Asta ignored her, too busy trying to break loose and get to Albert, who, as far as Myrna Loy was concerned, was hardly very enticing. Myrna surrendered. "Damn you, Asta, we'll go to Albert. Damn the torpedoes, full speed ahead." The dog strained at the leash and Myrna hurried to keep up with him.

Once at the photographer's side, Myrna watched in horror as Asta lifted a leg against one of Albert's legs. "Asta!" she shouted. "You little beast! That's unsanitary!"

Albert Garber stared down at Asta's performance and then spoke to the actress. "Minnie, don't you know I've got a wooden leg?"

"That's still no excuse for Asta to misbehave. We've done two pictures together and he's always been a perfect little darling. Asta! You apologize to Albert at once!" Asta stared at Myrna, whose unique and lovely nose was quivering with indignation. Then he turned to Albert and barked once.

"No offense taken, Asta," said Albert as he finally indicated to Myrna that she resume her position at the curb, "it's happened before."

Myrna led Asta to the curb while mumbling to herself, "Of all the dippy ideas of doing a shoot on Wilshire Boulevard when it could have been just as easy to do in the studio. And why am I so damned cooperative? Norma Shearer wouldn't participate in a stunt like this. What the hell is Hollywood's so-called perfect wife doing this in this awful heat!" She saw her maid, Teresa, coming from the studio van parked at the corner and bringing her what looked like a refreshing glass of lemonade. "Teresa, you're heaven-sent!"

"Hold it!" shouted Albert. The experienced actress froze, likewise the experienced Asta, and Albert Garber clicked away. The pictures would make their way around the world in newspapers and magazines, by way of wire services that fed Hollywood to the hungry universe. Myrna Loy was hot news. She was one of the ten top box-office stars, and had been ever since she co-starred with her pal William Powell two years earlier as the witty and sophisticated Nick and Nora Charles in *The Thin Man*. This year alone they had co-starred in three films, all winners. They were beginning the New Year with a comedy called *Double Wedding*.

But all was not well in Myrna's world. There was a husband to contend with since her marriage in June in Ensenada, Mexico.

They had lived together for four years before deciding at last to marry, four years during which she had walked out on him at least seven times, and only two weeks ago she had walked out on him again. Walking out on Arthur Hornblow seemed to be her favorite form of exercise.

"Turn your head to the left and look up. Let's get a good shot of that gorgeous nose!"

"Bugger my gorgeous nose. I need some of that lemonade." She took the glass from Teresa and swallowed a healthy swig. Now a smile played on her lips as she fluttered her eyelashes and looked warmly at Teresa. "Mother's milk, as Mr. Bernard Shaw called it." The drink contained a hefty belt of gin. Teresa took the glass as Myrna turned her head to the left and looked up. She paid no attention to the six members of the studio's private police force, who were holding back the small crowd that had gathered once word got around that the glamorous and glorious Myrna Loy was right here on Wilshire Boulevard posing for publicity pictures. Her mind was on the pretentious parvenu she had married, a successful producer and a damned good lover who considered himself a connoisseur of fine wines, who ate in only the very best restaurants and ordered his clothes from the artisans of London's Savile Row. This man who made her read fine literature and attempted to teach her everything he knew about history and historic architecture, Galatea to his Pygmalion.

Mother's milk indeed, thought Myrna as Teresa, reading her mind, brought the glass back to Myrna.

"Are we almost finished?" asked Myrna. "I've got a luncheon date at the studio and Mr. Powell hates to be kept waiting." She favored her fans with a smile and hoped to God they wouldn't mob her, though the six studio policemen were brawny bruisers and she had seen them handle crowds before.

"How's about picking up Asta and hugging him?"

"How's about picking up Asta and strangling him?"

Jean Harlow was pouting. Metro's blonde bombshell was the studio's best pouter. She was also very curvaceous and sexy and could take an ordinary line of dialogue and make it sound hilarious. Even while pouting. She sat on the couch in William Powell's dressing room watching him read a racing form and dope the selections at Hollywood Park. Her hands were folded in her lap as she said petulantly, "You're not paying any attention to me!"

"Of course I am, Baby." Myrna Loy was Minnie and Jean Harlow was Baby and amazingly enough, the two opposites in femininity were very good friends. "From the sound of your voice I can tell you're pouting. Why?"

"When are we going to get married?"

"Oh that. I thought it was something important."

"Why do you keep stalling?"

"What's the rush? You've already had more than your share of husbands. You mustn't be greedy." If he married her, Powell would be number four. "Heavens! You're only twenty-six and you've chalked up three marriages." He thought for a moment and then said, "I had no idea marriage could be habit-forming." He looked at his wristwatch. "I wonder what's keeping Minnie? It's past twelve-thirty. She's always on time. Maybe the shoot isn't going well."

"Albert Garber is a fussbudget." Harlow brightened. "Did you know he has a wooden leg?"

"Everybody knows he has a wooden leg. I'm sure by now Asta knows he has a wooden leg and delights in the knowledge."

"He tells everybody he lost it in the war. But that's a lie. His sister, you know, the one in makeup, she told me he lost it in a car crash."

"Aha! Wooden leg! That's a sign!"

The blonde sat up. "Are you going mad?"

"Right here in the third. Long John Silver! And the odds are very favorable." He wrote in a pad on the table at which he was seated.

"What about Long John Silver?"

"Have you never read *Treasure Island*?"

"I don't remember. Hey! Wait a minute! Wasn't that a picture a couple of years ago with Wally Beery and Jackie Cooper?"

4

Powell smiled. "Came the dawn."

"Came the dawn," she echoed. "Is that another horse?"

"No, Baby dearest, it isn't a horse. It's a cliché from silent films. Ah! You've stopped pouting! Now that's the way I like to see you." He crossed to her, lifted her in his arms, and gave her a kiss. He lowered her back onto the couch and studied her face. There was something about that beautiful face that now worried him. "Baby? Haven't you been sleeping well?"

"Why? Do I look tired?"

"Your eyes aren't sparkling. They usually sparkle."

"Don't worry. They'll sparkle when the camera's turning. Give me a cigarette." He flipped open the lid of a cigarette box and the dressing room was filled with a tinkly music box air. Powell sang along with it as he offered her a cigarette. " 'Let me call you sweetheart, I'm in love with you . . .' "

"That's real cute. What does your cigarette lighter play?"

"Some old torch song. When was the last time you saw a doctor?"

"I don't see doctors. We're Christian Scientists."

"Well, try a little Jewish science and have a check-up. I think you're run down."

"Daddy, you want to do something real healthy? Marry me!"

Myrna waved out the window of the limousine to her faithful fans as the car whisked her and Teresa back to the M.G.M. studios in Culver City. She looked at her wristwatch. "Damn. I'm going to be late."

"Is it urgent?" asked the chauffeur over his shoulder.

"I'm meeting Mr. Powell for lunch. He hates being kept waiting."

"We'll be there in ten minutes."

"That's impossible!"

"Miss Loy, just close your eyes and keep them closed until we get there. I guarantee you it'll be in ten minutes."

Myrna said to Teresa, "You shut your eyes too." Teresa's eyes were already shut. Asta, sitting in the front with the chauffeur, yawned and then whined as he felt the limousine suddenly gaining momentum. The chauffeur was bent over the wheel, now in imitation of the racing wizard Barney Oldfield, his idol. Myrna felt them rounding a corner on what she was sure was two wheels. She groped for Teresa's hand, found it, and clutched it tightly. Her heart was beating faster and she was positive her pulse was racing. She wanted to scream "Slow down!" but was positive by the time she got the words out of her mouth they'd be at the studio gate. She was almost right. They reached the studio in ten minutes flat.

"We're home!" announced the driver cheerily. "I'll take Asta to the kennel."

"You do just that. And thank you. That was quite an experience. On the way drop Teresa at the commissary. You all right, Teresa?" Teresa nodded but said nothing; her vocal cords were paralyzed. Myrna hurried from the limousine into the executive dining room. Powell hadn't arrived yet. Myrna exhaled, followed the chirruping hostess to the table, and en route paused to chitchat briefly with some fellow actors and several executives.

Louis B. Mayer was spooning his daily chicken soup, from his mother's recipe and a *spécialité* of the dining room. He sat with another executive, Benny Thau, who grunted when Myrna greeted him, a grunt being as gracious as he ever got. It was said of another producer who never missed church services on Sunday that he was holier than Thau. Mayer said to Myrna, "Make sure your chicken soup is piping hot."

Myrna stuck her chin out and said with a twinkle in her voice, "What makes you think I'm going to order chicken soup?"

"You don't want chicken soup?" He paused in midslurp, riveting his eyes to hers. She expected to hear him bark an order to have her stood against a courtyard wall in front of a firing squad.

"Not every day of the week I don't. Louis, why do I suspect that in addition to your stable of horses you've cornered the market in chickens?"

William Powell was suddenly at her side, his right hand clutching the racing form, his left arm surrounding her shoulders. "Ah, the perennial chicken soup. Mother's milk."

"Don't be ridiculous," said Myrna, "it's gin that's mother's milk."

Powell inquired archly, "Are you planning on a bowl of hot gin?"

"No, as a matter of fact, I'm thinking of chili with a lot of hot sauce." She said to Mayer and Thau, "You'll forgive us, won't you? We don't want to be late for lunch."

"Who's joining you?" asked Mayer, fearful it might be their agent, who always gave him indigestion.

"Nobody's joining us," said Powell. "We're both thirsting for a martini and I need a phone to place some bets."

Mayer snorted. "What do you know about doping horses?"

"I've never doped a horse in my life. I select my horses with great care. My bookie says I'm the most elegant horse selector in Hollywood."

Thau growled, "You got any tips?"

Powell winked at Myrna. "Long John Silver in the third at Hollywood Park."

"Ha!" ha'd Mayer. "Like the Stevenson character, that nag also has a wooden leg!"

"Oh really?" said Myrna. "I must tell Asta. He has a taste for wooden legs."

Powell yanked her away from the table and led the way to theirs. "Well, Minnie, it's been too long a time since we've lunched."

"Three days, for God's sake."

"That's much too long a time." Myrna smiled. She adored her friend. Not once since their first film together in 1934, *Manhattan Melodrama,* had he ever made a pass at her. Unlike Spencer Tracy and Clark Gable and director Victor Fleming, who never ceased to try to force their attentions on her. Her marriage to Arthur Hornblow hadn't dampened their enthusiasm, it just heightened the challenge. "How's Baby?"

"I just left her."

"Why didn't you ask her to join us?"

"Because I want you all to myself. Besides, Baby had to do some fittings. I don't think she's looking well." They were seated and a waitress had taken their orders for two very dry martinis with lemon peel. "There's no sparkle in her eyes today."

Myrna said wryly, "Maybe she's exhausted by your whirlwind courtship."

"Stop trying to fill me with guilt. Maybe she's exhausted by the constant demands of those two vultures she's living with."

"Now Bill," said Myrna, "that's no way to talk about her mother and her stepfather."

"They are vultures and they are bleeding her dry and they're not going to dig their talons into me and my money."

"Oh? Do you have much money?"

"Anything over ten bucks is much money to them." Myrna was studying a menu but paused to give Powell a mock stern look.

"Mama Jean adores Baby. So does Mario Bello." He was Mama Jean's husband, a suave Italian gigolo with a mustache not unlike Powell's. In fact, he somewhat resembled Powell as did two of Harlow's earlier husbands, the M.G.M. executive Paul Bern and cameraman Hal Rosson. Because of these resemblances, Myrna often found herself wondering if Harlow was looking for a stepfather figure. Paul Bern was mysteriously murdered just a few months after he and Harlow were married, but thanks to Mayer and his powerful political connections, Harlow's career survived the scandal.

Powell said, "I think that greaseball wishes Mama Jean was out of the way so he could have Baby Jean all to himself."

"How terribly astute you are," Myrna said as she buttered a roll. The waitress was serving the martinis. Myrna asked, "What took so long?"

The waitress adored Myrna and was used to her sometimes merciless teasing.

"The bartender had a hard time slicing the lemon peel."

"You sure he didn't try a pass?" He said to Myrna, "I tried a pass at her once and suffered a severely sprained wrist. She doesn't know her own strength."

"Oh yes I do. Ready to order?"

"I'll have the chili. With lots of hot sauce."

"No can do."

"Why not?" Myrna bristled with indignation.

"Mr. Mayer says you're to have the chicken soup."

Myrna suggested to the waitress what Mr. Mayer could do to himself.

Powell exclaimed, "Why, Miss Minnie Loy! I should wash your mouth out with laundry soap. To think a lady would say a thing like that. Let alone Hollywood's perfect wife."

Myrna waved her wrist at him disdainfully. "If you bring me chicken soup, I shall dump it on Mr. Mayer's head."

The waitress said, "If you do, I'll phone that in to Louella."

"Aha!" said Powell. "I've long suspected you were one of Louella Parson's spies. That's how she gets the stuff for that deadly column of hers."

The waitress leaned forward and took them both into her confidence. "You think we can live on the salary they pay us?"

Myrna leaned forward. "Got any hot tips for us? You know, some juicy little tidbit?"

Said Powell, "Like who's laying May Robson." Robson was a septuagenarian character actress who had been a reigning Broadway star at the turn of the century.

"If anybody's laying her," said the waitress, "we'd be planning her memorial service." She zeroed in on Powell pointedly. "But there's something cooking with Claire Young."

Powell lowered his martini. "What about Claire Young?"

"Well," said the waitress, basking in her brief spotlight, "I got the word today that Hollywood's busiest madam is sick and hurting for money."

"Claire's got the first buck she ever earned," said Powell.

"Yours?" asked Myrna innocently.

"Minnie, you must control that evil streak of yours." He asked the waitress, "Where'd you get this story?"

She straightened up and turned coy. "Well, Mr. Powell, that's for me to know and you to find out."

"Just for that, there'll be no tip."

"Honest, I can't tell you. I was just told to spread it, that's all."

Myrna said, "Spread it? Like an infectious disease?"

The waitress shrugged. "What do you want to eat, Mr. Powell?"

"Is there Virginia ham?"

"There's ham, but I'm not sure where they got it."

Powell and Myrna exchanged a look. Powell said, "I don't care where they got it as long as it's fresh."

"I heard tell it was so fresh, it talks back to you."

Powell put a hand over Myrna's. "We must not laugh. We must not encourage this tray bearer."

"Don't be mean, Bill. I've known her since I came to the studio four years ago, isn't that so, Cordelia?"

Powell flashed Myrna a look. "You mean she has a name?"

"Of course she has a name," insisted Myrna.

"Except it ain't Cordelia," said the waitress. "But you're close. It's Regan. My mother adores Shakespeare. Thank God my aunt Bertha talked her out of naming me Titania. Can you imagine what I'd have gone through in school with all the kids calling me Titty?" She decided this was a good exit line and headed for the kitchen to place their orders.

"Poor girl," said Myrna. "So underpaid." Powell's face was a study. "Is that dour look on your face due to Regan or Claire Young?"

"It's due to the thought of blackmail."

Myrna folded her hands on the table as she watched Powell drain his martini and then hers and signal for refills. "Claire Young has a reputation as a square shooter," said Myrna. "I can't believe she'd resort to blackmail."

"I've known a lot of people to do a lot of strange things under adverse circumstances. Maybe Claire doesn't have the kind of money I always suspect madams are supposed to have."

"Really, Bill. A madam is as human as the rest of us girls. She likes to spend money freely."

"How do you know how a madam feels?" Powell regarded her sternly.

"I happen to have a pretty darned good imagination. I mean can you imagine what kind of a life a madam leads?"

"Very organizational, I should think."

"Do you realize a madam is on call twenty-four hours a day?"

"You mean like a doctor?"

"Well, in their way they minister to the sick and needy. Claire told me Wally Beery thinks nothing of phoning and bellowing for service at all hours of the night."

"Why, Minnie, I'm about to go into shock, and then into a steam bath. You know Claire Young?"

"One of my minor accomplishments."

"How the hell did you get to meet Claire Young? And don't you dare shock or disillusion me. You may be Myrna Loy to the world and Minnie to your friends but you're my beloved Nora Charles to me and my Nora can do no wrong."

"I was doing right when I met Claire Young."

"Don't tell me you go the same church?"

"I don't go to church. I sleep late on Sunday, it's the only day of the week that I can."

"Don't change the subject."

"I didn't, you oaf. You did. I met Claire Young about three years ago. I was assigned *Penthouse* opposite your pal Warner Baxter. Although the script never came right out and said so, I played a call girl."

"Shame!"

"It was a damned good part. Anyway, I decided the part needed some research. So I asked Warner if he knew any call girls."

Powell was amused. "Did he?"

"First he had a coughing fit. I thought it was apoplexy but thank God it wasn't." The fresh martinis arrived, served by the bartender himself, an occasional privilege afforded the studio's biggest stars, and Powell and Loy were among the biggest. They thanked the bartender and then returned with alacrity to call girls. "Warner and I were lunching right at this table. We hadn't seen each other since we did *Renegades* for Fox back in '31."

"So Warner told you about Claire Young."

"Boy, did he tell me about Claire Young. Surely you know."

"Surely I know what?"

"She was once under contract here."

"She wasn't!"

"She was! I read her file and don't ask me how I got my hands on it, but I got my hands on it." She sipped her martini. "She was being groomed for stardom but she made one fatal misstep."

"Aha!"

"She had an affair with a very important producer."

"The name, Minnie, the name."

"It wasn't in the file."

"You're making all this up just to kill time until our food arrives."

"I am not! The studio nailed her on the morals clause we all have in our contracts and she was finished."

"The beasts."

"Indeed," said Myrna. "There was an inference that Mrs. Important Producer knew about the hanky-panky and got our Louis to lower the boom, which he did presumably to avoid any scandal. Despite the awful setback, Claire was obviously made of sterner stuff. From here on in I'm telling you what Claire told me."

"Why, Scheherazade, you have me hypnotized!"

She said jauntily, "I'm telling it beautifully, aren't I?"

"Why, you egotistical little snip."

"I'm too old to be a snip. Now drink your martini and let me get on with the story. Another producer offered to set her up in the prostitution business. Not as the madam, mind you, but as one of the girls. But Claire's got a lot going for her between her ears. This producer absolutely *loathed* Louis B. Mayer or so Claire said. So Claire said, 'Set me up in business as the madam and I'll recruit a lot of my girls from the Metro lot. That'll fix Louis B.'"

"No!"

"Yes, and close your mouth, you look very unbecoming."

"I probably need a facial. So go on, go on!"

"That's it. He set her up, she got her girls from here and certainly some of the other studios and she thrived, and how she thrived."

"My hat's off to her."

"When it's not your trousers." He laughed. She sipped her

drink. Then she asked, "Do you believe what Regan told us?"

He thought for a moment. "I don't want to, but someone seems awfully anxious to spread those words."

"Bill, I listened between the lines."

"And my precious Minnie, what awful thing did you hear?"

"You heard the same thing, my sweetheart."

"I'm feeling very dense. What did we hear?"

She tweaked his nose. "We heard a very nasty threat of blackmail."

T W O

$\mathcal{P}$owell reared back. "That's what I said a few minutes ago."

"You didn't sound sure of yourself."

"Well, I may have sounded a bit tentative. I always do when I'm not too sure of my suspicions." He looked about the room to give himself a moment's pause. "Why do Christmas decorations seem so out of place in this room?"

"Because we don't get any Christmas bonuses," retorted Myrna smartly. "Oh look! Woody's headed our way." W. S. Van Dyke II, Woody to his friends and co-workers, had directed *The Thin Man* and given Myrna her chance to prove herself as a comedienne despite strong studio opposition.

"I'm not asking you for an invitation to join you," said Van Dyke as he pulled out a chair and sat. "You look glowing, Minnie."

Myrna indicated her drink. "Second martini."

"Two at lunch? That's not like you."

"There may be a third. By which time Christmas might have disappeared."

Van Dyke feigned shock. "Where's your Christmas spirit?"

"I don't have any. I've every kind of spirit except Christmas. I've even got the spirit of '76. Want some?" She cocked her head to one side waiting for his reply, but she knew he wasn't interested in their frequent banter. "Woody, I think you're nursing a bad case of worrisome gossip."

"You've heard" — he leaned forward and whispered — "the Claire Young news?"

"Oh yes," said Myrna cheerily. "I prefer that to Christmas."

Van Dyke said to Powell. "What do you think? Do you think it's true?"

Powell replied matter-of-factly, "Why don't we phone and ask her?"

"Oh, I like that idea," said Myrna, still cheerily. " 'Hello, Claire. This is half of Hollywood's male stars calling you. Are you planning to blackmail us?' "

Powell said nothing. He was not amused. Van Dyke said, "I would never think that of Claire."

"You're thinking it now," said Myrna.

"Keep it up, Minnie, and I might belt you one," said Powell.

"No you won't, because I'm the only logical thinker at this table. She wouldn't dare blackmail anybody openly. She'd be sealing her doom." The men stared at her. "There'd be a contract for her and I don't mean for a featured role." She smiled at a writer who passed the table and winked at her. Myrna lowered her voice. "We know there's a certain someone in this room who's a past master at arranging to eliminate obstacles, human or otherwise. If Claire is doing anything at all, she's waiting for unsolicited contributions. I know I would if I were in her position."

"Well, you're not in her position," said Powell.

"Someday I might be." Powell snorted. Van Dyke chuckled while wondering if he could borrow a sip of martini from either one of them. "Besides, how do you know it's true? What you got was a piece of gossip from a waitress who makes no bones about being vastly underpaid. It's quite possible Claire doesn't even know what's going on. This could be the work of someone being malicious and spiteful and God knows this town is overpopulated with that kind of monster." She paused while seething. Then she remembered something. "Of course, there's her little black book."

A little black book was news to the men. Myrna's bombshell detonated quietly. She looked from one to the other while silently damning Van Dyke for sipping her martini.

"Exactly what little black book are you referring to, Minnie?" Powell fought hard to sound suave and self-assured, to keep his voice from wavering. Myrna took the opportunity to fill Van Dyke in on the circumstances that had led to her acquaintance with Claire Young. "Minnie." Powell bore down on the name. "You're not answering me." Before she could say anything, the waitress arrived with their food.

She asked Van Dyke, "Can I get you anything?"

"A good lawyer." He winced as Myrna kicked him under the table.

Said Regan, "We're fresh out. How's for some chicken soup?"

"Nothing for me," said the director, "I'm lunching at another table."

"All he's doing here is sip my martini. Bring me another and one for Mr. Powell too, because he's looking underprivileged."

Regan left, flashing them a look over her shoulder.

"Minnie, I hope I'm sounding sufficiently ominous to frighten the hell out of you." Powell's eyes narrowed but it only succeeded in making him look bilious. "The little black book."

Myrna said innocently, "It's Claire's. I don't have it."

"You know what's in it," Powell persisted.

"I know what Claire told me. She didn't show me it, she simply said she kept one." She looked from one to the other. They were not happy. "She said she kept a daily log of who availed themselves of her services."

Van Dyke groaned. Powell stared at the ceiling. Then he spoke, very softly, enunciating each word clearly and succinctly. "We'll be condemned from pulpits across the country. The Vatican will hurl thunderbolts at us. There'll be a display of hellfire and brimstone that will blind us and destroy us."

"Oh now really," scoffed Myrna.

"Minnie, must you be reminded of the morality clause in our contracts? There'll be no excuses accepted."

"I've used up most of mine," said Van Dyke.

"Why Woody Van Dyke, you devil you."

Powell said, "We will be ruined. We'll lose our homes, our careers, our women, and our friends in no particular order."

"You won't lose me," said Myrna staunchly. "And Baby will stand by you. Eat your ham. It'll get cold." She tasted her chili. "Not bad." She asked Van Dyke, "Want a bite of my chili?"

Woody said gallantly, "Anything but your chili." He moved to leave.

"If that's a *double entendre,* I choose to ignore it. Who're you lunching with?"

"Unfortunately, and under the circumstances, a very very young new actress. I'll stay in touch," with which he departed.

"Bill, eat your food. The brown sauce is beginning to congeal."

Regan brought the third round of martinis. "Will there be anything else?"

"Sanctuary," said Powell as he sliced himself some ham.

At eight that morning Claire Young, smartly dressed in a Chanel suit, had been sitting with her legs crossed, staring at Dr. Mitchell Carewe, who sat behind his desk toying with a letter opener. He was a handsome man in his early forties and Claire was thinking he resembled a mannequin in a department store window. Claire's earlier ingenue beauty had matured into early middle-aged good looks though she was not yet forty. Her face was carefully made up with the aid of a chart prepared for her by Perc Westmore, of the Westmore family of makeup wizards.

"Is that it?" Claire's voice was husky. She always saw the doctor at eight in the morning, before his nurse arrived, before other patients would be there to stare at her with curiosity and wonder who she was, if they didn't already know. Only her clientele and her staff knew her; the outside world recognized the name, but had no idea what she looked like. A few knew she'd been a Metro actress under another name, and pictures of her did exist, but they'd be hard put to match the face of the starlet of yesteryear to the Claire Young of today.

"I'm sorry, Claire. You told me to lay it on the line and that's where I've laid it. It's on the line. It's inoperable."

She opened her alligator handbag, found a cigarette case and lighter, and was soon lighting up. "How much time do I have?"

"If you'll stop smoking, you might have more than I predict."

"How much time?"

"It's not easy prognosticating these things."

"Try a wild guess. How much time do I have to put my house in order?" She smiled. "No pun intended."

He set the letter opener aside and folded his hands on the desk. Claire stared at his hands. Those beautiful fingers. Those long, slender fingers.

"I admire your guts," he said.

"You've always admired my guts. Come on, Mitch, stop horsing around. How much time?"

"Somewhere between six months and a year, give or take any sudden setback."

"Well, what do you know?" She blew a perfect smoke ring. "My last Christmas. Well well well." She thought for a moment. "I don't know if I can stand the pain. What will you do for the pain?"

"You can depend on me." He cleared his throat and then asked, "Are you having trouble sleeping?" He didn't wait for an answer. "I'll prescribe pills."

"I didn't ask for any."

"I'll prescribe them just the same."

"Why, Doctor." She feigned shock. "How unethical."

"Why unethical? Sleeping pills are always prescribed for patients who are having trouble sleeping."

"I didn't say I was having trouble."

He said intensely, "I love you. I'll always love you."

"Now, Doctor, that's no way to speak to a patient," she chided. "Don't love me, Mitch. Just be my friend and be my doctor."

The phone rang. Carewe lifted it to his ear. "Dr. Carewe." His face hardened. "You're a little early, aren't you?"

Claire stubbed out the cigarette. She could guess who was at the other end of the call. The doctor's gambling debts were legendary. He was a familiar figure at the illicit gambling clubs in Hollywood. She heard him say something rude and then slam the phone down.

Claire asked, "Still against the ropes?"

He said nothing, but busied himself writing a prescription. He tore the slip of paper from the pad and held it out to her. She took it and looked at the hieroglyphics he had scrawled.

"Christ! How do pharmacists decipher these things?"

"Claire."

"Yes?" She folded the slip of paper and tucked it in a pocket.

"The book."

"What book?"

He knew she knew what he was talking about. "What are you going to do with it?"

"I haven't given it much thought. I might take it with me." She laughed. "You want to buy it?" He said nothing. "In the right hands, it's worth a fortune." She had the door to the outer office open.

He stood up. "I know it's worth a fortune."

Claire stared at him. "You're not looking too good, Mitch. 'Physician, heal thyself.'"

Five minutes later she was behind the wheel of her modest Chevrolet. She guided it out of the garage under the building onto Wilshire Boulevard. Traffic wasn't as heavy as she expected it to be. Then she knew she had to pull over and park. *My last Christmas.* Her eyes were misting with tears. She fumbled in her handbag for a tissue. No tissues. She dug deeper and found a dainty handkerchief embroidered with lace. It looked so delicate it seemed a shame to use it, but she needed to use it. She dabbed at her eyes and, after a while, examined herself in the rear-view mirror. Still a good-looking broad. A good-looking broad who had just been handed a stiff sentence. She wondered if there really were such things as miracles. If there are, they're for other people, never for sinners. Never for a sinner like Claire Young.

The Chevrolet was back in traffic, headed for her modest house in Beverly Hills. Her modest house. Her modest Chevrolet. Her modest savings account. She'd never been good with money. She knew how to make it but she didn't know how to keep it. Money took precedence in her thoughts. Money. How to get more money in the short time allowed her. She spotted an M.G.M. van pulling into Rodeo Drive and parking at the corner as she paused for a red light. Probably doing a shoot. Rodeo was all decked out in its Christmas finery, almost as lovely and as pretentious as the ornaments on Wilshire. The department stores had outdone themselves in lavishness, and it was so goddamned hot. A horn tooted anxiously behind her. She wasn't aware the light had changed. She was aware only of Christmas decorations and a need for money. Money, she reminded herself, is the root of all evil. Well, she needed money and if need be she'd use a little evil to get it and bugger the consequences. She wouldn't be around to suffer them.

Claire's house was on North Alpine, a bit south of Sunset Boulevard. There were some movie star houses on the street, mostly married couples. Some of the men knew which house was Claire's. They had crossed her threshold often enough, but rarely remained longer than to have a drink and select a girl, Claire usually arranging for several to be on hand for inspection. Once a pair had been settled on, client and the lucky lady repaired to a hotel or a motel room or to the young lady's apartment if she had one. Claire didn't let her clients "buy blind," that is, have her send over a girl and pray she'd be something they wanted. They came to the house and chose for themselves. She prided herself that a few romances had blossomed and several had led to marriage, and a few times Claire had been invited to dinner or Sunday brunch out of gratitude.

She pulled into her driveway. She recognized the blue Buick in front of her. It belonged to her assistant and best friend, Fern Arnold. Fern had been at Metro when Claire was there and they had struck up a friendship that lasted until now, because Fern had stood by her during all the unpleasantness. Fern left Metro to dance in some Busby Berkeley musicals and then left those to work with Claire.

Fern Arnold had a pair of legs that made strong men swoon and women go sick with envy. In a corner of the beautifully furnished living room, Fern stood on a small ladder decorating a Christmas Tree. She was wondering what to do with a cherub ornament and was glad there was no one about to give her a suggestion. She heard the front door open and called out, "Claire?"

Claire answered unenthusiastically, "Yes, it's me."

"I don't like the way 'me' sounds."

Claire came into the room and removed her hat listlessly, throwing it on a chair. Fern held the cherub ornament against her right ear. "Does this do anything for me?" Her voice was warm and loving. Her eyelids fluttered as she waited for Claire's opinion.

Claire sank onto the overstuffed sofa, reaching for a cigarette in the box on the end table. She finally answered Fern while applying a table lighter to the cigarette. "It won't start a fad."

Fern had come down from the ladder. "You've got news for me and I can tell it's not good." She stood with hands on hips, staring down at Claire.

"No, it's not good. Stop staring at me like that or I'll start blubbering. It's inoperable."

"That's conclusive?"

"As conclusive as it can get. Park somewhere, honey, you're obscuring my view of the tree."

"It's just a Christmas tree like any other Christmas tree."

"It's a special Christmas tree." She took a long drag on the cigarette. "It's my last Christmas tree."

Fern stifled a sob. She sat next to Claire and hugged her. "What'll I do without you?"

"You'll have plenty to do. As executor of my estate, you'll be up to your hips in paperwork. You'll be okay. You could take over the service. The girls like you. They trust you. You've been with me long enough to know how to run it."

"I'll think about it." She sniffled and reached across Claire to a box of tissues. "Damn it, I had a feeling today was going to be a bummer."

Claire put her cigarette in a tray and then said straight out, "I need a lot of money, Fern."

"I'll give you what I've got, which is very sweet of me considering I don't have very much."

"I don't want your money, I want *their* money." She retrieved the cigarette, got to her feet, and took a puff.

"Who you talking about?"

"You know who I mean. The Johns. The clients. You still friendly with that Whatsername, the one who sells gossip to the columnists?"

"You mean Hazel Dickson?"

"That's the one."

Fern studied Claire. "What do you want with Hazel Dickson?"

"I want you to feed her some stuff that'll knock her on her backside."

"Hazel's got quite a backside."

"I want you to tell Hazel you hear tell I'm thinking of exposing the contents of my private diary. My little black book. In the form of a memoir."

"You wouldn't do that!"

"That's right, I wouldn't. But it ought to bring me a lot of Christmas checks. You know. Hush money. You've heard about hush money."

"I've heard about it, but I've never earned any." She said sadly, "There's never been any reason to hush me up." And then it hit her. "Claire, it's blackmail!"

Claire's hands were outstretched in supplication. "What do you want me to do?" she pleaded. "I've got no other assets. I've got no other means of raising money." She waved an arm over her head.

"This place is mortgaged up to the hilt. I'm not winning any popularity contests at the bank."

"Don't you know someone special with lots of money?"

"Fern, I know a lot of someone specials with lots of money. They've all been in this room at one time or another. And I expect these someone specials to do me something special."

Fern got to her feet, still clutching the ornamental cherub. "Oh God. You're putting your life on the line."

"For God's sake, it's already on the line. Now you listen to me and put all sentimentality aside. Just remember what my dear old granny on my mother's side told me in one of her rare moments of sobriety. 'Sentimentality and loyalty can be very expensive.' Now listen . . ." Claire was working on a fresh cigarette. "Tell your Hazel something like this. Claire's got a little black book. It's got names and dates. It could blow the lid off this town." She suddenly remembered. "You know, I've told very few people about the book. I told Myrna Loy."

Fern was startled. She dreaded to think why Myrna Loy had been privy to such exclusive information. Claire told her about Myrna researching the role of a call girl. Fern sighed with relief. "I thought you were going to tell me something awful about her. She's such a lady. She's one of my favorites. She has such good taste."

"There was a lapse in it when she married that horse's ass Hornblow."

Fern remonstrated. "He's such a gentleman, honey. He's so meticulous when he's selecting a girl for himself."

"And I'm tired of his asking, 'Is she vintage?' Pretentious son of a bitch. The hell with him, let's get back to Hazel." She embraced herself, feeling a sudden chill.

Fern asked, "You're sure you want to go through with this?"

"Come up with some other options, and I'll be grateful. But there aren't any." Another drag on the cigarette. She slipped her hand in a pocket of her jacket. The prescription. She wouldn't tell

Fern about it. She'd given Fern enough to worry about. Then her thoughts switched to Myrna Loy. A really sweet woman. The perfect wife. The perfect wife to an imperfect husband. She said to Fern, "I hear Myrna's walked out on Hornblow."

"I hope it's going to be a very long walkout. I wish she'd marry William Powell. They go so well together."

"Fern, you're not dialing. Come on, honey, get going on Hazel Dickson."

Hazel Dickson was sitting at her kitchen table listening to the uproar caused by a glass of Bromo-Seltzer. Damn Herb Villon for letting her drink those Brandy Bombshells at the Brown Derby last night. Herb Villon, detective first class, boyfriend second class, lover third class. She wondered if he had spent the night. She was too wrecked to go back to the bedroom and see if he was still there. She looked at the wall clock. It was after ten. If he'd spent the night, he'd have been long gone to his precinct downtown. She stared at the Bromo-Seltzer. She hoped there was enough strength in her hand to raise the glass to her mouth. There was. She downed the Bromo in one long gulp followed by one long unladylike belch. She screamed as the phone rang, startling her. "Steady, girl," she said to herself. "Steady. Just answer the phone. It's on the wall next to the stove. That's right, Hazel. One foot in front of the other one. You can make it, kid." She lifted the receiver. "Hello." Her voice was very faint.

"Hazel?" Fern's voice was strong and forthright.

"Hazel," said Hazel, wondering if she was the Hazel in question.

"Hazel, are you all right?"

"Hazel all wrong."

"Hazel! It's me! Fern Arnold!"

"Edward Arnold?"

Fern said to Claire, "I suspect a monumental hangover." She returned to Hazel. "Fern Arnold, Hazel, Fern Arnold. I've got a hot scoop for you."

Hazel's eyes widened. The words "hot scoop" always sobered

her up when she needed sobering up. "Yes, it's me. I'm Hazel. How are you, Fern?"

Fern said, "This is an exclusive, Hazel. It's yours and yours alone."

"I love you, Fern. Right now you're the marines and the Royal Canadian Mounted Police come to the rescue. Listen, I'm in the kitchen. Let me get to my desk in the living room. There's something to write on there."

"Go ahead."

"Don't hang up!" She let the receiver dangle. Living room. Where's the living room. She blinked her eyelids rapidly to force her eyes to focus. Straight ahead. Living room. She drew her blue dressing gown with the marabou trim tightly around her and then staggered to the living room. She made it to the desk and lifted the receiver. "You there, Eddie?"

"Fern!"

"Fern! Fern! Right. Okay, shoot." She picked up a pencil and drew a stenographic pad closer to her.

What she heard sobered her up.

"Fern, is this for real?"

"So help me God."

"This could turn Hollywood into a ghost town. They'll be making all-girl movies. Oh Fern, this is worth a fortune to me." She thought for a moment. "It could be worth a bigger fortune if I could have a look at the book."

"Maybe later."

"There's really a book, Fern?"

"As real as Claire Young." She put her hand over the mouthpiece and asked Claire, "Do I tell her about you-know-what?"

"Don't you dare!"

Fern spoke into the phone. "Claire, you'll get this to the right people?"

"In this town, all the right people are the wrong people but I predict it's going to make me a bundle. And you'll get your finder's fee, honey. Thanks, Fern, from the bottom of my heart, my genuine thanks. I've been having a really rough time."

"This ought to smooth things out. If you need me, I'm at Claire's."

Within the next ten minutes, Hazel Dickson had racked up over ten thousand dollars, feeding the little-black-book hot potato to a variety of gossip columnists, beginning of course with the queen of them all, Louella Parsons. Hazel knew how to make the item even hotter. She got on the phone to several of her spies, especially Regan, the waitress who worked in the M.G.M. executive dining room, who soon spread the gossip through the room.

While Hazel worked her telephone overtime, Fern prepared a pot of coffee in the kitchen to where she and Claire had repaired.

"Okay, Claire," said Fern, as she also consigned some slices of bread to the toaster, "the fat's in the fire. Prepare yourself for the flak."

"I'm all prepared. My will is with my lawyer. He knows how to reach you. You know how to reach him. He knows how to get to my Aunt Maidie."

"How is it over at Maidie's?"

"It's fine. Soon it'll be better." The coffee was perking. "I'll be right back."

Claire went to the phone in the living room and dialed. She snapped her fingers impatiently. Soon she heard, "Amelia Hubbard."

"It's Claire. You free for some dictation?"

"Hallelujah, am I ever. When do you want me?"

"Five minutes ago."

"I'm on my way."

Claire returned to the kitchen, where Fern was buttering the toast. "Amelia Hubbard's on her way here."

"What's up?"

"Why, Fern honey, I'm going to prepare another bombshell. I'm going to dictate my memoirs. The black book is for names. The memoirs are for real." She looked at Fern. "In for a penny, in for a pound."

Fern shrugged. "Why not? Just make sure you spell my name right."

"I'll make sure I'll spell everybody's name right. Especially Louis B. Mayer's."

THREE

After lunch, Powell and Myrna went to her suite in the building that housed the stars' dressing rooms. Myrna rated something special along with Garbo, Norma Shearer, Joan Crawford, and Jean Harlow. She sat at her dressing table, fussing with her hair, while Powell paced back and forth behind her.

"Bill?"

He was preoccupied.

"Bill!"

"What?"

"Do you think my ears stick out?"

He stared at her ears.

"Well, do they?"

"I'm giving them my undivided attention. Hmm. Who told you your ears stick out?"

"Photographers have been telling me that ever since I started in films back in the dark ages. Albert Garber said it this morning when he was photographing me for that *Vogue* spread."

Powell said, "I never get asked to do any spreads."

"You were in *National Geographic* fly-fishing. How many actors get to be in *National Geographic*?"

"Along with the baboons and orangutans."

"Well? Do my ears stick out?"

"Nothing like Gable's."

"Well, I should hope not." She examined her reflection in the dressing table mirror. She said firmly and with much conviction, "Well, I think my ears are adorable."

"Your ears are priceless. And there's a knock at your door. Probably Baby. She's always hoping to find us in a compromising position."

Myrna said as she walked to the front door, "Shall I act all flustered and embarrassed?"

"Don't you dare! I don't need you adding to my problems."

Myrna opened the door and Harlow walked in wearing a bathing suit Adrian, the M.G.M. designer, had created especially for her. She walked past Loy and then past Powell with arms outstretched, as though on display on a runway. She asked, "What do you think this does for me?"

"Too much," said Powell.

"That's what I told Adrian. Of course he disagreed with me. At the top of his voice. Myrna? This thing do anything for you?"

"I certainly don't have a body like yours."

"Well, I hate it. Myrna, can I borrow a robe?"

"In the closet. Help yourself." The closet was behind a lovely Chinese screen where one could change clothes discreetly if there were others in the room.

While she struggled out of the bathing suit, Harlow said with rare wickedness, "Popsy? Have you heard about a little black book?"

Without missing a beat, Powell said, "Of course. It's called the Bible."

"I heard this was some other kind of bible with some other kinds of Philistines, the Hollywood sort."

Myrna marveled at Powell's lack of discomfort. In films he had raised poise to an admirable position as a rare form of art. "Baby, you shouldn't waste your valuable time thinking about little black books."

"These days I've got precious little else to think about." Harlow selected an emerald green dressing gown and came out from behind the screen while tying the sash.

Powell said, "How dare you sashay across the lot in that bathing suit?"

"Would you prefer I sashayed naked? I only came over to get your opinions. I've got to go back for some more fittings. I wish to hell I was qualified for something other than the movies."

"You could sell blouses in a department store," suggested Powell.

"For the kind of money *that* pays? That wouldn't buy Mama Jean a pair of stockings."

Powell said to Myrna, "Don't you get the feeling Mama Jean's stockings are spun from gold fiber?"

"Well, they ain't," snapped Harlow.

Powell persisted, "Perhaps your Mama could step into your shoes and sell blouses."

Harlow said, "She wouldn't know where to begin. She's never worked a day in her life."

"Pity," said Powell.

"Now what about the little black book?"

Myrna inquired winsomely, "Isn't there a nursery rhyme about a little black book?"

"Not one that I ever learned," said Harlow. "Now listen, you two. I got it all from Woody Van Dyke and what he left out that waitress Regan filled in. Now come on, you two, stop giving me a hard time. I've got to know if my stepfather's in it and how much it's going to cost me."

"Have you been told he's in it?" asked Powell.

"Well, if he ain't," said Harlow, "it'll be a first to celebrate. He's scratched at the door of every cathouse in Los Angeles. I can't believe Claire Young is a blackmailer."

"You'd be hard put to make that accusation stick," said Myrna.

"How so?" asked Powell.

"An item of gossip isn't actually blackmail." She was buffing her nails. "I think this one in particular is a subtle suggestion by the lady that she's a bit strapped for cash and all contributions would be accepted agreeably."

"Nicely reasoned, Mrs. Hornblow. But have you considered what fresh cans of peas are about to be opened, if they haven't already been opened?"

Harlow asked, "What have peas got to do with this?"

"I adore peas," said Myrna, "especially cooked in a cream sauce with sliced mushrooms and sprinkled with paprika."

Powell said smoothly, "Class will come to order or there'll be an outbreak of knuckle rapping. What I had in mind, ladies, is that this sort of thing could be an invitation to murder."

Harlow asked, "What's murder got to do with a can of peas?"

"It's merely a metaphor, Baby." He patted her cheek gently while noticing again the grayish pallor of her usually porcelain-white skin. "And stop putting on the dumb act, we know you've had a couple of years of college."

Myrna placed the buffer on the dressing table top. "Bill, you think Claire Young might be murdered."

"Well, I've certainly been entertaining the thought."

"Now really, Bill . . ." said Myrna.

He said smartly, "I like making all the money I make. I like my beautiful house and my cars and taking Baby to expensive restaurants. Hell, woman, I've worked my butt off for years to get all this!"

Myrna said, "That's a strong case. Go ahead. Kill her."

"I'll be your alibi!" volunteered Harlow.

"There you go, Bill. You're all set. Choose your weapon." Loy was captivated by the glow on Harlow's face. That's true love, Myrna told herself, that's genuine true love. Bill won't do better. He'd be a fool not to marry her.

"It's got to be the perfect crime," said Harlow.

"Oh, absolutely perfect," agreed Myrna.

"I'm delighted you two are enjoying yourselves." Powell looked at Harlow. "You didn't really cross the lot in that outrageous garment?"

She laughed. "Of course not. I brought it back to my suite and put it on there." She was on her feet. She crossed to him and kissed him. "I've got to get back to the fitting room. Myrna, I'll bring the robe back later."

"There's no rush, Baby." She went to Harlow, took her hand and led her to the door. Harlow's fingers were ice cold. And it was such a warm day. At the door, they embraced.

"See you later!" said Harlow airily and she was gone.

Myrna asked, "Bill, is she well? Her fingers are icy cold."

"There's something wrong there. The color of her skin isn't right either. Oh well, it's probably another one of her colds."

Myrna said, "She's had at least four this past year. What she needs is a complete check-up and I'll phone Mama Jean and tell her so."

Powell was lighting a cigarette. "Have you forgotten so soon, Mrs. Hornblow? They are Christian Scientists. They don't believe in doctors."

"I hope they believe in dentists. I'd hate to think of them nursing swollen jaws for an eternity. Asta was a perfect little beast this morning."

Powell brightened. "You went to see the little fellow?"

"He was part of the shoot. Asta and me in an M.G.M. chinchilla coat in the sweltering heat on Wilshire Boulevard. They *would* assign a photographer with a wooden leg."

Powell put a hand over his eyes. "I know what's coming."

"Exactly," corroborated Myrna, "I was so embarrassed. The photographer, Albert Garber, wasn't. The studio should pay for the dry cleaning."

"You think of everything, don't you, mommy." He tweaked her nose. "When do you and your lord and master kiss and make up?"

"He's not my lord and master, which is the seed of the problem. And as for being kissed by him, like his precious imported wines, he prefers me at room temperature. The hell with him, do you suppose Louis has heard by now?"

"Indubitably. There's probably a council of war underway in his office right now. Many tears on his part ending with a fainting spell. The man should have been an actor."

In Louis B. Mayer's office, he was flat on his back on a couch, eyes closed with Benny Thau kneeling at his side and slapping a wrist. He looked knowingly at Howard Strickling, the head of publicity, who sat in a chair stifling a yawn. In a chair beyond him, her elbows on the desk and her hands propping up her motherly face, sat Ida Koverman, Mayer's wise assistant and hatchet woman.

Benny asked his recumbent boss, "Louis, can you hear me?" He turned to the others. "I think this one's real."

Ida Koverman snorted. "They're never real." Strickling chortled. Koverman looked at him, thinking, He knows where all the bodies are buried because he put most of them there.

Mayer's eyes were open and glaring at Koverman. "Ida, you're fired." Thau helped him to sit up. Koverman sat back in her chair and examined some fingernails. They were blood red. She might have been tearing at somebody's throat.

Koverman said, "What about Claire Young?"

Mayer was on his feet, raging about the immense room. "She's doing this for revenge! Revenge, I tell you! Revenge!"

Strickling said, "After all these years she's getting around to revenge?"

"Why not? She was a pretty smart kid. Now she's older so she's probably smarter."

Strickling reminded Mayer, "Louis, Claire Young's operation isn't exclusive to M.G.M. I'm sure there's a lot of eyeball rolling and chest thumping over at Warner's, Twentieth, and Columbia."

Mayer asked, "You're telling me her clients are stars? Nothing but stars?"

"Not exclusively," said Strickling. "Also some featured players, directors, producers, writers . . ."

"And I suspect some Seventh-Day Adventists," said Ida dryly.

"You shut up!" snapped Mayer. "I told you you're fired!"

Koverman raised a leg and straightened a stocking seam.

"You know, Louis, if there are some players you're looking to drop, you can always exercise the morals clause," Strickling said.

Mayer's face lit up. "Of course! The morals clause."

"That's right, Louis," said Koverman. "You can get rid of Wally Beery, Bill Powell, Robert Taylor, Gable, Walter Pidgeon . . ."

The thought of dropping all his big moneymakers made Mayer clasp his hands in front of him and look beseechingly at the ceiling. His eyes erupted with tears and Koverman said under her breath, "Oh Christ, I should have known."

Mayer said through what he hoped were heart-rending sobs, "We'll be finished! There'll be no more M.G.M.!" Benny Thau, handed him a tissue. The sobs subsided as he dabbed at his eyes.

"Howard," demanded Mayer in a cold voice, "what are you going to do about Claire Young?"

Before Strickling had a chance to reply, Koverman interjected, "Louis, shouldn't you discuss this with Zanuck and the Warners and Harry Cohn? . . ."

"What!" Mayer raged. "I should let them know I'm worried?"

"Louis," said Koverman, "they know you're worried. They know everybody's worried. Even Asta is worried."

"That mutt goes to a whorehouse?" He pronounced it *hoorhouse*.

"That mutt eats from the *Thin Man* series," said Koverman. "Instead of sitting around on our duffs waxing dramatic, we should start worrying about what it'll do to the box office. If this inflates into a woozer of a scandal and names get named, they'll be condemning us in every church around the world, and that's an awful lot of movie patrons except in darkest Africa."

Mayer shouted, "Howard!"

Strickling said, "We've got to get our hands on the book."

"If it's in a safe-deposit box, all is lost," said Koverman.

Strickling scoffed. "You think she runs to the bank every time she wants to jot something down in that damned book?"

Mayer glared at Benny Thau. "Well, Benny? Have you nothing to suggest? You just sit there like a statue?"

Thau said softly, "Kill her."

★

Only in the rarefied atmosphere of the circus known as Hollywood could an Amelia Hubbard create herself. She was a public stenographer exclusively to the studios and the stars. It was her secondary profession. Her greatest claim to fame was that she was the most recognizable female extra in films, right up there with the indomitable Bess Flowers. They were the elite of extras known as Dress Extras. They had accumulated over the years extensive personal wardrobes, mostly acquired cut-rate but still in good condition from local thrift shops. Happily these clothes were largely movie star hand-me-downs and therefore had very impressive labels. Dress Extras provided their own clothes when on call and frequently looked more impressive than the stars. They were on call for elegant party and dinner sequences, for weddings, and as members of opera and theater audiences. They were recognizable to audiences, albeit anonymous, because directors selected them to surround the stars and enhance the scene. Sometimes they were given a line or two to speak, which increased their paychecks. Usually they were seen saying to their hosts, "It was a *lovely* evening" or "Next time at our house!" unless the fictional hosts were royalty.

Amelia was another refugee from the M.G.M. studios along with Claire and Fern. Amelia's problem was her height. She stood five foot nine in her stocking feet and most leading men were anywhere from five six to five eight. In her brief sortie as a featured player, Amelia was always either seated or lying on a divan. If the scene positively required her to stand, either a small trench was dug for her to stand in or the actor stood on a box. Amelia soon realized her days in front of the camera were numbered, so she wisely enrolled in a secretarial school and just as wisely let directors and casting directors know that extra work was not beneath her. Being both proficient and well liked, Amelia was soon profiting from two careers. Unfortunately there often were dry spells when work in both areas slackened off and her current dry spell was a very dry one.

Claire and Amelia were working in Claire's bedroom. Fern was downstairs manning the phones, which required very little attention now that word of the little black book had gotten around. Amelia's long legs were crossed and her stenographer's pad rested on her knee as Claire dictated in fits and starts. When Claire was sure of her thoughts, there'd be a steady flow of words. But frequently there were long pauses while she contemplated censoring herself. Several times Amelia blushed. She was neither a prude nor a prig, not with her tenure in Hollywood, but much as she had heard about the town's bacchanalian orgies, she'd never heard about them in such shocking detail.

"Oh come on now, Amelia. All your years in this town you're telling me you've never been to an orgy?"

"All I know about orgies is what I've seen in C. B. DeMille and Erich von Stroheim epics. But for crying out loud, smearing peanut butter and jelly all over a girl and then . . . My God, kids eat peanut butter and jelly sandwiches all the time!"

"That's where it begins," said Claire matter-of-factly. "Wait till I get to the chocolate sundaes. Where was I?"

Amelia read aloud: "An invitation to an orgy at Lionel Atwill's home in the Hollywood Hills is more sought after than an invitation to the White House."

"Okay, I remember." Claire lit a cigarette, exhaled, and then resumed dictating. "The men were stark naked and hopping about the ballroom on all fours. The women straddled them, beating their backsides with leather strips provided by the host. It was like a rodeo with the men trying to buck like broncs and the women hanging on to their necks to keep from falling off. At one orgy there were two heart attacks and one stroke in addition to a few nosebleeds."

"God," said Amelia.

"Don't editorialize," cautioned Claire. "Atwill's orgies were very elegant. One of the girls told me John Barrymore stood stark naked on the ballroom balcony twirling sparklers while reciting a soliloquy from *Hamlet*. He moved her to tears."

"Claire, you don't really expect this to be published? If it is, these people could sue!"

Claire might have said, I don't give a damn. If this thing is published and they sue, I won't be around for the trial. She knew it wouldn't be published in her lifetime. But having these personal memories committed to paper was as important to her as the black book and its list of assignations and participants. The phone rang. She knew Fern would get it and if it was important, she'd buzz her.

Amelia was thinking, John Barrymore naked and twirling sparklers. It's a wonder he didn't burn himself. She heard a buzzer and watched Claire pick up the phone.

Dr. Mitchell Carewe was trying to control his anger though the tongue in his mouth was on the verge of becoming blisteringly uncivil. She had barely said hello when he asked, "Have you gone out of your mind? Putting the black book on the market!" He didn't wait for an answer. "Do you know what it could do to me?"

"I haven't the vaguest idea what it could do to anyone."

His words blistered her ear. She took a drag on her cigarette and winked at Amelia, who was thinking Claire was an incredible woman. She told Amelia about her cancer as though she had a date to play cards. Though she knew the news shocked and sorrowed Amelia, she got right down to the business at hand with alacrity and enthusiasm. It was as though her death sentence had given her the freedom to unlock her inner self and dig deep into and release the hidden resources of strength and power she had sequestered for so many years. She heard Claire saying, "Are you finished, Mitch? I'm giving dictation to Amelia."

Amelia knew that 'Mitch' would be Dr. Carewe. Now why would a nice guy like Dr. Carewe be giving Claire a hard time? This led her to dwell exclusively on the doctor. So charming. So distinguished-looking. So expensive. She'd seen him once about a minor ailment on Claire's recommendation and she could still remember the thrill of his touch. It had been a long time since she had filed in her memory some thrilling touches.

Claire said, "I promise you, Mitch, you have nothing to fret about. After all, my dear Mitch, my death is in your hands."

Amelia winced.

Carewe said, "I believe you, Claire. But what you're doing, it's so unlike you."

"No it isn't, Mitch. It's just another face of prostitution." Claire hung up the phone, took a last drag on the cigarette, stubbed it out in the ashtray, and said, "Now for Mr. Louis B. Mayer."

fOUR

Hollywood was awash in emergency conferences. Producers conferred with stars, stars conferred with their agents, wives conferred with wives as to what action they should take against their husbands, if any, and mistresses considered socializing with men in other professions than acting. *Maître d's* conferred with chefs, gossip columnists conferred with their editors, and on it went. Lillian Hellman, in Hollywood with her lover, Dashiell Hammett, creator of *The Thin Man,* dubbed the studios the League of Notions. And amazingly enough, Claire Young was oblivious of the emotional earthquake she had created.

A conference of another kind was taking place in a Chinese restaurant called the Doll's House. It was situated on Fairfax Avenue off Wilshire and owned by Jimmy Woo, a man in his thirties who was always quick to confide that he was actually a Mandarin prince descended from an emperor nobody had ever heard of and therefore could not check up on. The food was extraordinarily good and inexpensive, and detective Herb Villon, who lunched there at least once a week, suspected that Jimmy Woo had another source of income from the clandestine opium trade that Villon knew had escalated in Los Angeles during the past five years.

Villon was at a favorite table with his long-time and long-suffering paramour, Hazel Dickson, and Villon's assistant, detective Jim Mallory, who was a shy and reticent man prone to harboring a variety of passions for a variety of actress. Four years earlier they had been involved in a case with Marlene Dietrich and Jim was still recovering from his case of unrequited love, ignoring the song lyric that said unrequited love's a bore. The three were attacking a plate of assorted appetizers, though Hazel was favoring a concoction whipped up for her by Jimmy Woo, who guaranteed it would obliterate her hangover, a recipe Woo said was handed down through the centuries from a woman ancestor who had claimed she was raped by Marco Polo, her reputation saved by a Mandarin emperor who had a taste for damaged goods.

"I don't understand Claire doing this," said Villon, munching on a sparerib.

"I do," countered Hazel knowledgeably.

Villon eyed her with suspicion. "Are you responsible for starting this emotional epidemic?"

Hazel said matter-of-factly, "Claire started it. She had Fern Arnold toss the ball to me and I went for the touchdown. I'm making lots of bucks."

"Swell," said Villon, "now you can pay me back the C-note you borrowed too long ago." She ignored the statement. Hazel was always borrowing from him and never paying back, looking on the money as a much deserved bonus. "Okay, Hazel, so why is Claire killing the golden goose?"

"The goose isn't golden. It's the eggs she lays." Hazel was feeling much better and her appetite had improved. She was working on a second helping of appetizers, even though aware there were several succulent main dishes to follow. "I've known for a long time Claire's been hurting for money. She's not as smart a businesswoman as Madam Frances and those other flesh dealers. They take a fifty-fifty cut. Claire does seventy-thirty, the thirty for herself."

"That's pretty dumb of her," said Villon.

"She claimed it got her a better class of girl." Hazel was attacking a lobster roll with a fork and Jim Mallory winced. She had a policy of showing food no mercy and Herb and Jim were well aware of it, but her table manners were execrable. Dining with a star she was Dainty Daisy personified, even taking the precaution of dabbing at her chin with a napkin to catch any dripping juices, rather than working her tongue like a windshield wiper which she was now doing.

"Golden eggs or no golden eggs, Claire's shot herself in the foot."

"That's too bad," said Mallory. "Claire's always been good to me."

So that's where he got his jollies, thought Villon. Well, he's young and vigorous and he's got to let off steam somehow. As attractive as he was, Villon never knew him to have a steady girl-friend.

Mallory continued with a shy smile on his face. "She knows a cop gets paid *bubkes* so she always gave me a discount."

Villon asked, "Did she throw in some cookies and a glass of milk?" Mallory's cheeks flushed.

Hazel said to Villon, "Lay off. A discount is a discount."

Villon had had his fill of appetizers and lit a cigarette. "I suspect there's something not too kosher about this move. You realize Claire's putting herself on the spot. Just about every actor in this town has a short fuse. Somebody might be planning to take a shot at her. Hazel, have you discussed this with Fern Arnold?"

"Haven't had the chance. But I don't have to. Fern is true blue where Claire is concerned. They've been pals for years. Fern would lay down her life for Claire."

Villon flashed her a look. "Cut the melodramatics."

"It's not melodramatics. It's an honest fact, as plain as the cleft in your chin. I've known Fern a long time. She's pretty good about feeding me stuff."

"And she fed you this dynamite about Claire." They watched a waiter clear away the dirty dishes and another waiter serve the main courses. Hazel bent forward and inhaled extravagantly.

"Don't fall into the moo goo gai pan," cautioned Villon, who frequently had to rescue Hazel from asphyxiation when she'd had one Stinger too many. Jimmy Woo hovered nearby and Hazel said, "Jimmy, you've outdone yourself."

"For crying out loud, you haven't eaten any of it yet," said Villon.

Jimmy Woo said, "She doesn't have to. All she has to do is smell it. A true epicure."

Hazel looked at him with gratitude while Villon stubbed out his cigarette and Mallory loaded a plate with lobster in oyster sauce. Jimmy Woo went to greet some fresh arrivals.

Herb said to Hazel, "Take it from your boyfriend, Herb Villon, whose own sense of smell makes him an epicure of another sort, this little black book smells to me like an invitation to blackmail."

Mallory said, "I don't think blackmail is very inviting."

Villon said to him, "Don't eat with your mouth open. It makes you look like a cement mixer."

Hazel asked, "You mean by going public about the book she's really announcing she's open to all bidders?"

"You're catching on. The way she's done it is very safe."

"What do you mean 'safe'?"

"This way is very subtle and I admire her for it. No threats, no oral or written demands, she's clean. If somebody is dumb enough to try to lower the boom on her without something in writing that he can show us, we have to say to him 'When you unzipped your trousers she wasn't holding a gun to your head.' " He finally began to fill his plate. "This is going to be very very interesting."

"It's already interesting," said Hazel. "Oh, how I wish I was a fly on the walls of some executive offices."

Jim Mallory was about to speak but remembered first to swallow his mouthful of food. "I know you, Herb. We've worked together a long time. You think Claire Young is marked for murder."

"You're good, Jim. You're close. Claire Young and murder are skipping rope together." He paused to sample his food. "I think Claire Young has marked herself for murder."

"Oh go on!" said Hazel. "You mean she's inviting somebody to do her in?"

"It's a possibility. Look at it my way. All of a sudden from out of nowhere a cathouse madam announces her little black book might be up for grabs. We can attach a lot of meaning to that. Number one, she needs money, so boys, somebody better fork something over, preferably a lot of somebodies. Number two, she's genuinely going out of business and wants to feather her sparse nest with some much needed eggs. Number three, there's an unknown factor behind her need for money."

"What unknown factor?"

"Like maybe she's seriously ill. It's a conjecture, but a possibility. She doesn't think she's going to make it. She wants to leave somebody comfortably fixed."

"Like who for instance?" asked Hazel, nursing a thought that what Villon was theorizing could be shaped into another profitable exclusive for Louella Parsons.

"Maybe she's got some guy she's been supporting. Fern ever mention any guy?"

"I never tried to look into the possibility of some guy in Claire's life. Anyway, all the madams I'm acquainted with have deplorable taste in men. They usually have a toothpick sticking out of their mouths, suck their teeth, and inhale when their noses are running. If Claire has a guy, I'd like to think he has some class. Claire's a pretty classy lady."

"She's a damned classy lady," seconded Mallory.

Villon said to Hazel, "How many times have I told you discounts can breed loyalty?"

Hazel asked, "You want a discount?"

"For what?" asked Villon.

"For nothing," said Hazel. "I'm eating the rest of the lobster. Aren't you guys interested in the pork fried rice?"

"I never found fried rice interesting," said Villon. "I find Claire Young very interesting."

Hazel asked, "You trying to tell me in all these years you've never tested the waters at Claire's?"

"If you're expecting me to tell you anything about my private

43

life, such as it is with you for a girlfriend, you're going to have a long wait. Jim?"

"Yes?"

"How'd you come to hit it off with Claire Young?"

"Just plain lucky," said Jim with a smile of self-satisfaction.

"What are you going to do now that Claire's about to become yesterday's news?"

"I'll tell you after I consult my ouija board." He switched his attention to the fried rice. Hazel was suddenly absorbed in two middle-aged men within earshot at the next table. One was bald, the other had the kind of high-pitched voice favored by birds and dogs. The bald one was admonishing his friend. "You should show Jimmy Woo more respect. He's royalty. He's been a prince for over thirty-five years."

"So what?" piped his friend. "I've been a queen for over forty."

Hazel said to her friends, "Don't you just love Hollywood? Hey, Villon!" She snapped her fingers. "Come back to us."

"Hmmm? Oh, sorry. I was thinking of Jim's remark about Claire Young being a damned classy lady. In my experience with classy ladies, they're never anything but classy. Even classy madams." He thought for a moment. He asked Hazel, "Didn't Claire begin as an actress?"

"At Metro. She got nipped in the bud by a jealous wife of a big-shot producer who was hotly smitten with our Claire, or so the story goes. The wife went to the very top, to the very moral Louis B. Mayer, very moral as in ha ha ha, and the outraged Mr. Mayer rid not only the studio but the profession of Claire Young. Except that wasn't her name then and don't ask me what it was because I've never bothered to find out. I did try to find out who at Metro convinced Claire she'd be a good madam and financed her, but Claire stayed clammed up."

Herb Villon asked, "Couldn't Fern tell you?"

"Not old true blue. Actually I did ask her and she swore she didn't know and besides, she implied he's long gone from Hollywood."

"He probably is," said Villon. "Or else Claire would have gone to him for the money she seems to need."

"Herb, that makes absolutely good sense," praised Hazel.

Villon had a fresh thought. "I wonder if Louis B. is in the book."

"Him? Don't be ridiculous. He's too smart for that and besides, he's got a vast harem established in his own territory. He doesn't have to go looking for an outside nosh. Howard Strickling keeps him provided with more than enough bed mates. Louis B. doesn't try to make it with his stars either, though it's said he got Grace Moore in return for a two-picture contract back in 1930, both disasters. There was one star he truly loathed and destroyed — Mae Murray, back in the silent days. And he's not particularly nuts about Harlow, but she's too big at the box office for him to turn nasty. He's lending her to Zanuck for *In Old Chicago* in return for Tyrone Power in *Marie Antoinette*."

Villon raised his eyebrows. "He's going to play *Marie Antoinette?*"

"Oh, for crying out loud, Herb. Norma Shearer's Marie."

Jim Mallory spoke. "Do you suppose Claire has it in for Louis B. Mayer?"

"Oh, I'm sure she does," said Hazel.

Villon interrupted. "You go back a long way with Fern Arnold, don't you?"

"Over ten years."

"You knew Claire then too?"

"Need I remind you that was not her name back then? And if I knew her by any other name, I absolutely don't remember." She slammed her hand on the table. "Hey, wait a minute!"

The waiter clearing the table froze.

Hazel said to the waiter, "Not you, dear." He resumed clearing. "Herb, I may be on to something. Fern did mention a friend who was involved with somebody who worked in a hospital. Hmmm. Now let me think. Something like a lab technician or an anesthetist. Is there such a thing?"

"There is indeed such a thing. You think Claire might have been this friend?"

"It's a possibility, isn't it?"

"Worry your brain a little harder. There's got to be a big reason for Claire to need big dollars."

"By the way, what are you giving me for Christmas?"

"I've given it no thought. Damn it!"

A startled Hazel yelped. "You almost gave me a heart attack!"

"Me too!" said the squeaky voice at the adjoining table.

"Sorry," said Herb while Mallory signaled a waiter for a fresh pot of tea.

Hazel asked, "Damn it *what?*"

Herb said quietly, "I think Claire is looking to get herself killed and for the same reason she had Fern get to you with the scoop on the little black book." He paused and looked from Hazel to Mallory and back to Hazel again. "I think it's a very strong possibility she's been told her days are numbered."

"Isn't that what you said before?"

"No. I said I think she's looking to get herself killed. And I think the reason why is that she has a terminal disease."

Mallory wore a pained expression. "Gee, Herb, that's awful."

Hazel said, "But it's possible. God, if so, what an item!"

F I V E

$\mathcal{G}$riselda's Cage was a charming bistro on Hollywood Boulevard adopted by New York's writing and acting refugees. It shared equal time with the bar of the Garden of Allah Hotel on Sunset Boulevard where most of New York's displaced hung their hats. Griselda was a failed New York playwright who had migrated to Hollywood when the talkies began and succeeded in becoming a failed Hollywood screenwriter. She was a delightful woman who sadly lacked a gift for writing. But she was an excellent cook and at the urging of her husband they managed to cobble together enough money to open the restaurant. It was an instant success and they never looked back.

William Powell and Myrna Loy sat with Dashiell Hammett and Lillian Hellman in a booth over which hung an imitation Tiffany lamp. The illumination did a lot for Myrna but very little for the homely Miss Hellman, who would have preferred to make do without any illumination whatsoever. People who knew both the gifted and successful writers could never understand Hammett's attraction to Lillian, he being tall, slender, and handsome. He was looked upon as a man of the world, though Hellman was hard put to figure out which world, the old world or the new world. It took a lot of patience and hard work to get to know Hellman, if one was at all interested in knowing her. She was as tough as brass, sarcastic, and rude, but despite these shortcomings enjoyed a wide circle of friends, all of whom never wanted to know what she really thought of them. Hammett had provided Powell and Loy with *The Thin Man,* a film that was shot in only sixteen days under Woody Van Dyke's hasty but brilliant direction, with a script by the Albert Hacketts, whose dialogue was far wittier than that in the book. Hellman insisted that Nora Charles was fashioned after her and this was possible if one exercised a wide stretch of the imagination.

Each had a very dry gin martini with a twist of lemon in front of them, and the Tiffany illumination made the martinis sparkle like diamonds. Myrna commented, "They're so lustrously pretty, it's almost a shame to drink them. Of course on the other hand, there's more where these came from." She lifted her glass. "I'd like to propose a toast. Here's to Claire Young, a woman who I doubt has much of a future but she sure has one hell of a past." The others raised their glasses and drank. "All right, Bill. You had an audience with the pooh-bah himself," meaning Mr. Mayer. "Did he weep, did he faint, or did he offer you chicken soup?"

"Well actually, Mrs. Hornblow, he assured me that regardless of the outcome of this sordid scenario, my morals clause would never be exercised and that after you and I complete *Double Wedding,* he wants me to co-star with Joan Crawford in a remake of *The Last of . . .*"

". . . *the Mohicans,*" said Hellman swiftly, feeling rather pleased with herself but not for too long.

". . . *of Mrs. Cheyney,*" said Powell, punctuating it with a very disdainful sniff.

"Oh, I'm so glad it's that dated old warhorse. I can't imagine you as Hawkeye or Uncas," said Hellman.

"Thank you, Lillian. You made that sound like an epitaph," said Powell, downing the remains of his drink and signaling for another round, which caused Myrna to mouth him a kiss. Powell acknowledged her gratifying gesture with a smile and more information.

"We discussed Claire, of course, and he went to great lengths to assure me he never knew the woman. After which I went to great lengths to remind him that she was once under contract to the studio under another name. I think my great lengths outpointed his great lengths because he became, for Louis B. Mayer, unusually flustered."

"He didn't attempt to swoon?" asked Myrna mercilessly.

"Well, for a second there I did think his eyes were about to roll up into his head, but I think the last time he pulled that fainting stunt on me I doused him with a very handy pitcher of water. Actually, what he did I found rather admirable."

Hellman folded her arms and said, "Louis B. Mayer never did anything admirable in his life."

Powell said sternly, "Now see here, Lily. This is my story and if I say he did something admirable, then that's what he did."

"Okay," she retorted, "but I don't have to buy it."

"You most certainly don't," Hammett said, "because he wasn't offering it for sale. It was a simple statement of fact."

"Thank you, Dash," said Powell. "Now may I continue?" The fresh round of drinks arrived and the waiter distributed them rapidly and without spilling a drop. He collected the empty glasses while Powell continued his dissertation. "Mayer called in Ida Koverman and went into one of his dramatic specialties." He said to Hellman, "He has a vast repertoire of those things." Powell now gave a splendid impersonation of the Metro mogul. " 'Ida . . . no . . . no, don't sit, you won't be long enough for that . . . Bill says Claire Young was once under contract to us.' And Ida in her usual jocular manner, if you can stand her usual jocular manner, asks, 'What was?' At this point, Mayer's eyes narrow into ominous slits and he spits every word, 'Do a check on that.' Ida makes what for her is a swift departure." He explained to Hammett and Hellman, "Miss Koverman tends to lumber a bit."

Myrna interrupted him. "Hey, wait a minute! Didn't Ida ask what her name was when she was under contract?"

Said Powell, "Consider one of your precious cheeks delicately pinched." Myrna looked pleased while Hellman said under her breath, "Oh brother," and zeroed in on her martini. "While Ida was gone, all of I think a record-breaking three minutes, Mayer assured me no one could ever replace me as Nick Charles."

"Hear, hear," said Hammett.

"And me too, hear," added Myrna. "Lily, don't you agree?"

"Well, there's always Mickey Rooney."

"Why yes," said Powell, "there always is, isn't there. May I continue? Thank you. Mayer says we'll weather the scandal if there's a scandal to weather and besides, can you be sure this little black book really exists? I told him the only thing I'm sure of is death and taxes and he asked me not to be morbid. At which point Koverman comes slogging back into the room with a piece of paper. It seems that ten years ago or so there was a sweet young thing named Audrey Manners, Ida reading the name on the slip of paper. She was with Metro some six months or so and there was cause to exercise her morals clause. Why? Ida had no idea." Powell added, while indicating Myrna, "Minnie and I know."

"Well?" Hellman sounded very impatient. Powell told them about the producer and the wife who blew the whistle while Myrna studied the menu and was delighted to see pot roast and potato pancakes. "Anyway, I then asked Ida, aren't there any photographs of Audrey Manners in the files? And she said, 'I didn't bother looking. The files get cleaned out every few years.' "

"Baloney," said Myrna. "I was in those files looking for some photos of myself taken the first time the studio signed me back in '25."

"My God," said Hellman, "you've been around that long?"

"Longer," said Myrna airily. "In my early teens I danced in the stage prologues at Grauman's Chinese."

"Child labor," said Powell.

"You're damn right," said Myrna. "I was a child and those prologues were a lot of labor. You take my word for it, those files are intact. I even found a shot of me in *Ben-Hur*."

The information seemed to impress Hammett. "You were in *Ben-Hur*?"

"I was an extra in the chariot race sequence."

"I'm impressed," said Hammett. "Who were you rooting for?"

"No one in particular," said Myrna, "it was so damn hot out on the back lot, I was probably rooting for the director to yell *Cut* so I could go get a glass of cold water."

Powell interrupted her. "I insisted Ida send one of her flunkies into the files and ferret out a picture of Audrey Manners. Well, my friends, it seems that anything referring to Audrey Manners has been obliterated, or so the flunky told Ida."

"You don't believe that?" asked Myrna.

"Of course not. I then asked Mayer, did he think Claire might be marked for obliteration."

"Why do you use such big words?" asked Hammett.

"Because in this town, I rarely get a chance to use them."

"So there!" said Myrna.

"For crying out loud," said Hellman, "you two should be married to each other."

Hammett said with great sincerity, "Lily is right. There's a unique chemistry between you two."

"Oh please," said Myrna.

"Shut up, Minnie, and let the man continue." Powell flashed his teeth at Hammett. "Do go on, Dash."

"Christ," said Hellman.

Hammett said, "This is truly heartfelt before I have another martini and sink into a well-earned silence. You *do* have an amazing chemistry. You bring out the best in each other. In both *Thin Man* pictures, your rapport is magical." He turned to Hellman. "Go ahead, Lily, shoot me down in flames."

"I will not," she said, kissing his cheek. "It's the sort of eulogy appropriate to a double funeral."

"Okay, Hammett," said Powell, "I'm picking up the check."

Hellman, after lighting a cigarette, asked with her usual candor, "You mean to tell me you two have never had an affair with each other?"

"There was never any time," said Myrna. "You people don't seem to understand what a Hollywood contract entails. Do you know my first year under contract I did six pictures?"

"Dear God," said Hellman.

"Dear God, indeed," echoed Myrna. "There was a period when I acted in three films at once. Bill wasn't here then, he was still at Warner's. I'd work on one film in the morning, grab a sandwich, and work on the second film in the afternoon. Then a bowl of soup — no, not chicken — and head for picture three for most of the night. Thank God I'm a quick study or I'd have gone berserk. Now do you understand why I went on strike last year for more money and fewer pictures? They replaced me in *The Emperor's Candlesticks* with Luise Rainer and then threatened me with Roz Russell and a new girl named Ruth Hussey . . ."

"But the fans would have none of them," said Powell proudly. "They wanted Minnie and only Minnie and now they've got her forever."

Hellman growled, "Where the hell'd you get that nickname?"

"That's nothing. My husband calls me Queenie."

"Queenie?" Hellman was aghast. "That's a name for a Pekingese!"

"Oh really? Do you suppose my husband is trying to tell me something? I often think I lead a dog's life. If I remember correctly, Arthur insisted *he* was leading a dog's life. I wonder if Arthur's in Claire Young's book." She answered her own question. "I hope so. He hates to be left out of things."

"If he is in it, will you leave him?" asked Hellman.

"I've already left him."

"No!"

"Don't you read the columns?"

"What columns?" asked Hellman, thirsting for a refill.

"The gossip columns!"

"Hell no. I'm still ploughing through *War and Peace.*"

Powell could see Hellman was parched and had signaled for another round. "I didn't know anybody read *War and Peace.* I thought it was just talked about."

Hellman said, "I suppose Hornblow will do for a first husband."

Myrna was at a loss for words. Powell came to her rescue. "Why, Lily, there are lots of respectable first husbands in Hollywood.

Some of my best friends have been first husbands. And I thought I was a pretty good first for Carole."

"Carole?" queried Hammett.

"Why yes. Haven't you heard of Carole Lombard?"

"Oh yes. I read somewhere you just did a picture with her. Something about a forgotten butler," said Hammett.

"Not quite, but you're close. It's about a forgotten man who becomes a butler. *My Man Godfrey.*"

Hellman was puzzled. "You did a movie with your ex-wife? Wasn't that awkward?"

"Not at all. It was an excellent script and an enjoyable experience." A thought hit him. "Say! Carole would be perfect casting as Claire Young."

Myrna gave it some thought. "Carole as a madam? I don't think she'd go for that."

"Of course she would," insisted Powell. "She's got a vocabulary that would bring a longshoreman to his knees."

"You two are a pair of ghouls!" Hellman was truly appalled. "Why, the poor woman is hardly cold in her grave."

"Lily," said Powell.

"What?"

"She's still alive."

"Oh. Of course. Well, that makes it twice as ghoulish."

"Ah!" said Hammett as the waiter arrived with four martinis on a tray.

As he served the drinks and retrieved the empties, the waiter told them, "Griselda has asked me to tell you about our two specials. There's a very lovely Hungarian goulash and pot roast with potato pancakes."

"I'm for the pot roast," said Myrna. The others chimed in with their orders with only Powell opting for the goulash, thinking in Hellman's honor it should be spelled *ghoulash.* Myrna said to Powell, "Bill, did Louis B. mention getting together with the other studio heads to do something about Claire Young?"

"You know, Minnie, with hindsight, I now realize that there was a devil-may-care attitude about him. As though he knew this situation would be resolved to his satisfaction."

"Oh please, Bill, don't!"

"Please Bill don't *what?*"

"You make it sound as though he knows she's going to be killed."

"No comment."

"That's so cold-blooded!" said Myrna. She said sternly, "Bill Powell, it's your duty as a good citizen and a friend of Claire Young to warn her that her life could be in danger."

"Minnie," he said with exaggerated patience, "I should think by now you realize our Claire — "

"Your Claire. Not our Claire," said Myrna. "I've never met the woman."

"Yes you did," he reminded her with glee. "She helped you learn how to be a call girl."

Lillian Hellman feigned shock. "When were you a call girl, Myrna?"

"Oh, damn it. It was for a movie."

Powell wagged a finger at her. "You're behaving like all the rest."

Myrna waxed indignant. "What do you mean by that?" she demanded.

"You want the curtain permanently drawn on your brief affiliation with Claire Young. You think it might be harmful."

"I don't think that at all. It was a slip of the memory because I don't think that brief occasion is of any importance."

"Well then," said Powell, "why don't we phone Claire and invite her to join us for dinner?"

"I'd love to meet her," said Hammett, expecting Hellman to explode.

She disappointed him and said, "I'd love to meet her too. I once had a beer with Polly Adler." Adler was New York's most celebrated madam who at the height of her success had enrolled in a series of literature classes at a local university.

Myrna was annoyed. "You're treating her like a freak. She's a human being, not a sideshow, despite her notoriety."

Lillian said, "Myrna's right. Let's not ask her to join us."

Hammett said, "She probably wouldn't want to join us. She knows we're a disreputable lot."

Myrna chirruped, "Oh good! Here's our dinner!" Two waiters descended on them with the trays of food and the delicious odors were intoxicating. In their wake came Griselda Cage, the proprietor, followed by a third waiter with a tray holding a bottle of red wine and four glasses.

Powell was the first to espy her. "Why Griselda Cage, is that wine for us?"

"Courtesy of the house and a chance for me to meet Miss Hellman and Mr. Hammett and to bring you the bad news, Bill."

"What now?" he asked as she supervised the pouring of the wine.

"Long John Silver was an also-ran, just like in the book." She explained to Hellman and Hammett that this Long John Silver was a racing horse. Powell sighed sadly and then introduced Griselda to Hammett and Hellman.

"Pull up a chair, Griselda, join us."

"Not for long. I've got a heavy night." She borrowed a chair from an adjoining table. "So what's the latest buzz on Claire Young?"

"If there's anything new on Claire Young," said Powell, "I'm sure you're the one to tell us." He leaned toward her conspiratorially, "I know all about your grapevine."

Griselda's laugh was deep and hearty. "Believe me, Bill, it's vastly overrated. Sometimes Hazel Dickson lets me in on something juicy but that's about it. She was in last night with her boyfriend, Herb Villon, the detective. She told him plenty but she told me nothing."

"And who is Hazel Dickson?" asked Lillian.

"She's a go-between," said Griselda.

"And what does she go between?" asked Hellman.

"Lily, she's a liaison," said Myrna. "She marries items of gossip to the right columnists. She's a very celebrated young lady in this town. She's the best and the busiest gossipmonger there is. Drinks a little too much but then who among us dares cast the first stone?"

"This wine is delicious, Griselda," said Powell. "Very heavy, very fruity" — he looked at the impressive label — "and very very." He showed the label to Hammett and Hellman, who smiled their appreciation. "Minnie, would you care to examine the label?"

"No, thank you. I'm not much for examining labels. I've been put off them by a husband who prefers examining wine bottle labels to examining me."

"Now Myrna, Arthur adores you," protested Griselda.

"Not as much as he adores himself."

Powell said, "I move we change the subject. Let's get back to Hazel." He asked Griselda, "I suppose Hazel had the scoop on Claire Young."

Griselda shrugged. "You can't tell by me. She didn't mention a thing last night while she was still in a mentioning condition."

"Very possibly she didn't have the scoop last night," said Powell. "All hell didn't break loose until lunchtime today. We first got it from a waitress in the executive dining room . . ."

"Very classically named Regan," added Myrna. "Oh Griselda, this pot roast is heavenly."

"Made it myself," said Griselda with pride. "My grandmother's recipe."

"And who was your grandmother?" asked Powell.

"My grandfather's wife."

Powell asked Hammett and Hellman, "Don't you find this conversation scintillating?"

"Bill, behave yourself," cautioned Myrna. "I admire women who can cook. I can't, and thank God I earn enough money to hire one."

Hellman said, "You pay for the cook? What about Hornblow?"

"He criticizes."

"Charming," said Hellman.

"Not very," said Myrna. "We run through a lot of cooks."

"Lily's one hell of a cook," volunteered Hammett proudly.

"Dash, you lucky devil you," said Powell.

"Don't overdo it, Bill," said Hellman. "Look at him. Thin as a rail. Picks at his food. Look at what he's doing to his pot roast." She asked Griselda, "Doesn't he upset you?"

"Anyone who can write the way he does can do anything he likes with my pot roast."

"Is that a *double entendre?*" asked Powell.

"Not meant to be," said Griselda. She said to Powell, "Is all hell about to break loose?"

"Meaning Claire?" asked Powell. Griselda nodded. "All hell has already broken loose and I suspect shall continue to break and loosen for many a day to come."

"Hell. This means a lot of people are going to get hurt."

"Not necessarily," said Powell. "There are those who will undoubtedly fall by the wayside, but they were always meant to fall by the wayside. I suspect some of the studios will exercise the morals clause to cut loose actors already marked for termination."

"You'll be okay, won't you?" Griselda was genuinely concerned.

"I'll be perfectly fine," said Bill, "or I'll become a snitch."

"Cossack," said Hellman and then stoked more goulash into her mouth.

"Snitch on who?" asked Myrna. "Or should I have said whom?"

"Don't ask me," said Hammett. "I'm just a writer. We never know which is correct, who or whom."

"Out with it, Bill, who are you thinking of victimizing?" Myrna wasn't distracted from her pot roast.

"Snitching isn't victimizing," said Powell indignantly, "snitching is tattling. And if anyone gets my dander up, I just might identify some choice members of Claire's clientele."

"Such as?" asked Myrna.

"Oh, let me think. How about Lionel Barrymore?"

"Oh, don't be ridiculous," laughed Myrna. "He's too crippled with arthritis to be of any use to a prostitute."

"My dear Minnie, it's supposed to be the other way around. The prostitute is supposed to be of use to Mr. Barrymore."

"William Powell, you should absolutely be ashamed of yourself unless you're kidding us. You *are* kidding us." The smile on his face was the familiar wicked one. And then just as suddenly, the smile disappeared. He saw two people entering the restaurant, a man and a woman. Myrna succumbed to her curiosity and turned to see what had wiped the smile from Powell's face.

"Who are they?" asked Myrna.

"The woman is Fern Arnold," said Powell. "She works for Claire. They're pals from a long ways back. I don't recognize the man."

Griselda identified him. "He's a doctor. In fact, he happens to be Claire's doctor. Mitchell Carewe."

"My dears," said Myrna, much taken with Carewe's good looks, "I am considering changing doctors."

"Why?" asked Hellman. "He looks like a floorwalker in a department store."

"Oh well," said Myrna with an artificial sigh, "another illusion shot down in flames." She watched as they were seated in a booth at the opposite side of the room and after giving a waiter their drink orders, engaged in what seemed to Myrna's practiced eye to be a very heated conversation.

"Minnie," said Powell in a cautionary voice, "it's rude to stare."

"So stop staring," retorted Myrna.

Hellman pushed her plate aside. "You two have got to be married. You simply have got to be married. You behave more married than any marrieds I know." She stared at Fern and the doctor. "I don't think those two like each other."

S I X

$\mathcal{D}$r. Carewe was torching the cigarette in Fern Arnold's mouth while saying, "I'm doing as much as any doctor can do for Claire."

"Shouldn't she be in a hospital?"

"For what reason? Her cancer's in remission. She's been in remission for close to two years now. She's been luckier than most."

"How come now you tell her it's inoperable?"

"The remission is over. That's what her tests and examinations showed at Mount Sinai. It's spreading. I promise you, I told her as gently as I could. Fern, we know so little about cancer. I could put her into radiation again but I don't think she can take it. You know what the side effects did to her the last time."

"I know what they did to me," said Fern sadly, "sitting up nights with her and holding her in my arms." She flicked ash into a tray. "Oh what the hell, she doesn't want to live. She doesn't want to fight."

"She's set the town on its ear with her bombshell. Everybody's talking."

"Yeah, well I bet they ain't saying much."

"Where does she keep the little black book?"

Fern leaned back and took a drag on the cigarette. "I wouldn't know. Why do you want to know?"

"Curiosity. If there is a book . . ."

"There is."

". . . then it contains a lot of names familiar to me. The book's worth a fortune."

"And as usual, you could use a portion or a share of it. Claire says you're in to the boys for a very big bundle. You charge some pretty ritzy fees. Don't tell me you can't scrape enough together to pay off those mobsters."

"I'll level with you, Fern. I'm in way over my head. I'm drowning."

"Don't expect me to send flowers."

"Why do you hate me so much?"

"I don't hate you. I reserve hate for special occasions. I don't like you because of what you put Claire through. She didn't have to have an abortion." Fern stared at the glowing ember at the tip of the cigarette.

"I didn't know she had one. This is news to me!"

"Don't hand me that!"

"I swear, so help me God, I swear!" He seemed genuinely upset. "Did Claire tell you I was involved in an abortion?"

"She said something about being very ill when she gave you the air. She had to go to the desert to recuperate. She was laid up for months." She thought for a moment. "Maybe that was the seed of the cancer."

Carewe said knowledgeably, "A lot of Hollywood ladies have taken to the desert during the past few years. Off the top of my head I can name Constance Bennett, Miriam Hopkins, Loretta Young . . ."

"What about them?"

"They went to the desert to recover from serious illnesses and when they returned, each one brought a baby they'd adopted." He smiled, "Or so they said."

Fern said, "When you phoned to ask me to meet you, you said it was urgent. I haven't heard anything urgent."

"I want to marry Claire."

"Oh come on . . ."

"I've never stopped loving her. I never married, because no one could compare to Claire."

"If you're so hot to tie her up, why haven't you put it to her?"

"I have. Many times. Only this morning I told her how much I still love her."

"You love the little black book." He said nothing. "You want me to say a good word for you, is that it?"

"She listens to you."

"Sometimes. You know, I never knew why Claire turned to you when she first got sick."

He said adamantly, "Because I'm one of the best there is and as Claire told me herself, three doctors she consulted recommended me."

"I can't fight that. That's what she told me." After a moment she said, "Funny. Claire isn't one to hold grudges, unless you're Louis B. Mayer. Mitchell, no matter what I say, Claire isn't going to marry you. I was hoping you phoned me because maybe there was a possible option open to Claire. You know, like maybe one of those clinics in Switzerland I'm always reading about in *Liberty* magazine. Where they perform miracles, giving back youth to the aged, giving back health to the terminally ill, making death keep its distance." Suddenly her face was wreathed in a warm smile. "Why hello, Mr. Powell, fancy meeting you here."

"There's nothing fancy about me or this place. How are you, Fern?"

"I'm surviving." She introduced the men and moved over to make room for the actor to sit.

"I can only stay a minute. I'm with friends. Or at least they say they're friends." He told them who he was with. He said to Carewe, "Are you by any chance wealthy?" Fern suppressed a whoop. It didn't escape Powell, who said to the doctor, "I didn't mean to get personal on so brief an acquaintance, in fact, embarrassingly brief, but you see, and I'm sure you'll find this most flattering, Minnie — that's Myrna Loy — finds you terribly attractive and if by some strange means that leads to anything, I want to make sure you're well heeled enough to support her in the style to which she intends to remain accustomed. Of course Myrna is quite well off in her own right, as of this week, but she has a husband who has been a drain on her financial resources despite the fact he pulls down large sums of money as a producer. But he has this peculiar trait of preferring to spend her money rather than his own. They've only been married about six months now but for four years before the marriage they did live in what the gentlemen in the pulpits refer to as 'mortal sin' as opposed, I suppose, to 'immortal sin,' if there is such a condition." He swiftly abandoned Carewe, who bored him, and asked Fern, "And how is Claire?"

"Bearing up."

"Bearing up to what? We're the ones who should be bearing up. Now that she's unofficially announced that she's out of business, and shame on her without even holding a clearance sale. She *is* out of business, isn't she?"

"Why, you looking for some action?"

"Good grief, no. I've had a day heavy with action. I'm sure Claire is aware that the little acorn she fed Hazel Dickson has sprouted into one gigantic oak of a mess." He said to Carewe, "I'm sure you've heard of Claire Young's little black book. The world's heard of it by now, I'm sure. I'm sure it's wiped the Dalai Lama off the front page of Tibet's Lhasa Gazette, if such a periodical exists. But of course you've heard, you're Claire's doctor."

Carewe said, "You know an awful lot, Mr. Powell."

"I travel in excellent circles. But unfortunately I feel as though I'm going around in circles. Tell me, Fern, you have easy access to Claire's confidence, is this sudden ploy of hers a cue for those of us who have partaken of her services — that is, the services she has offered — to offer some sort of financial remuneration to keep her trap shut? That is, those of us who assume we're mentioned in this book. Am I in the book?"

"I don't know. I've never read it."

"Does it exist?"

"It exists."

"You know, Fern, there are a great many men in Hollywood, some of them terribly influential, who think Claire is indulging in a very subtle and, I might add, very dangerous form of blackmail."

Fern shrugged.

Powell asked, "Do I interpret your not too eloquent shrug as meaning 'yes' blackmail or 'no' blackmail?"

Fern said, "A shrug is a shrug."

"Add another 'is a shrug' and we might try attributing it to Gertrude Stein." Powell said to the doctor, "Have you any word for Miss Loy?"

"Yes," said the doctor, " 'Speak for yourself, John.' "

"I'm already spoken for. A lovely little lady named Jean Harlow." He returned to Fern. "As I said a few seconds ago, I'm sure Claire is aware she's playing a very dangerous game. I like Claire. Try to make her aware she could be sitting on a powder keg."

"Mr. Powell, you're not threatening her, are you?"

"Of course I'm not threatening her. I am Chicken Little bringing to her attention that the sky is falling." A waiter finally arrived with drinks. Powell said to the waiter, "What kept you?" He said to Fern, "Goodbye, Fern. Don't look so troubled. As my doctor said of a troublesome kidney stone, 'This too shall pass.' Goodbye, Doctor, though I think you're shameful for having thrown over Myrna Loy without even meeting her." He departed jauntily while Carewe and Fern quickly made use of their drinks.

At the other side of the room, Myrna said to Hellman and Hammett, "I wish I had studied lip reading. When I was an extra here way back when, I got very friendly with Lon Chaney."

"Oh, what a wonderful mime he was," said Hammett.

"Absolutely," agreed Myrna. "He offered to teach me lip reading and the sign language, because both his parents were deaf and dumb."

"You're kidding," said Hellman.

"No, it's the truth. But I thought it was his way of making a pass at me and back then I was Virginia the Virgin who didn't trust men because my mother told me not to and of course Mother knew best."

"Like hell she did," said Hammett.

"Like hell she still doesn't. Della May Johnson Williams, that's mother's dull identification, still doesn't trust men, or anybody else for that matter, although she likes Hornblow. I'll bet she's over at the house in Hidden Valley right now with Arthur."

"What's the house in Hidden Valley?" asked Hellman.

"It's a house I spent a fortune building for Arthur and me."

Hellman leaned forward and growled, "And I suppose it's in his name?"

"Oh no, it's in both our names." Hellman winced.

Hammett said in a voice coated with astonishment, "You walked out leaving him to live in the house?"

"Well, he had nowhere to go. He doesn't belong to any club or anything like that. So he booked me into the Chateau Marmont. It's quite cozy and quite reasonable, and talking about cozy and reasonable, here comes our friend Bill."

Powell sat and told Myrna, "You don't in the least bit interest him."

"What are you talking about?" asked Myrna.

"The doctor. Carewe, I believe is his name. I asked him if he might consider marrying you and the brute was noncommittal. He did say, 'Speak for yourself, John.' "

"But your name is Bill," said Myrna. "The man is terribly confused. I've lost all interest in him. I couldn't be interested in a man given to confusions. Well, did you learn anything?"

"Maybe, but I couldn't figure out what." He recapped his conversation with Fern and Carewe fairly accurately.

"Dear me, Bill," said Myrna. "I must admit it does sound as though you were making a threat to Claire. Now if she's murdered, will that Fern person finger you as the most likely suspect?"

"That wouldn't be very sporting of her," said Bill.

"Mr. Powell," said Hellman, "there's nothing very sporting about murder. You do agree, don't you, Dash?" Hammett didn't dare disagree.

Powell said suavely, "Has coffee been ordered?"

"Yes it has, and right on cue, here comes Griselda with a waiter in town. I hope he's not Greek."

"What makes you think he might be Greek?" asked Powell.

"I didn't say he might be, I said I hoped he isn't." They stared at her. "Well, you know, 'Beware of Greeks bearing gifts.' "

"He's bearing coffee and what looks like four snifters of brandy."

"They happen to be gifts. From Griselda."

"Well, that's very sweet of Griselda." She arrived with the waiter. "How very kind you are, Griselda. I assume this is your best brandy."

"Bill!" Myrna was shocked.

Griselda was laughing. "It's cognac from our private stock."

"Ah! Dash and Lillian . . . are you suitably impressed?"

Hammett raised his snifter to Griselda and Lillian voiced her thanks. The room was packed and the buzz of voices had assumed the volume of bomber engines in full flight. Griselda sat next to Powell, who managed to make a bit of room for her, a spare chair being unavailable. She said, "Well?"

Powell asked innocently, "Well, what?"

Griselda gestured with her head. "Those two over there."

"Fern and the doctor?" asked Powell.

"I saw you move in on them."

"I didn't move in, I just visited. Griselda, you look so serene and peaceful."

"That's because I have no time bombs to worry about. I couldn't hear what was being said, but from the look of it you had both of them worried."

"Oh, good for you, Bill," said Myrna smartly. "What was worrying them?"

"I think what worries Fern is that this whole little black book plot could backfire. It certainly smells of blackmail."

"To high heaven," said Myrna.

He told Griselda that Fern had taken much of what he said as a threat against Claire's life.

Griselda said, "I'm sure there's a small army amassed by now interested in seeing Claire done away with."

"Well," said Powell, "there's one damn good reason they better not do away with our Claire, not just yet anyway."

"I don't think they should do away with her at all," insisted Myrna. "I'm against capital punishment. Aren't you, Lillian?"

Hellman replied, "I'm against punishment but I'm all for any form of capital, which should squelch the rumor that I'm a fellow traveler."

"My dear people," Powell said, "let's stop being cute and adorable and take a sober look at the situation, though with all the booze we've consumed there might be a difficulty. The one damn reason to keep Claire alive is this: to make sure the book doesn't fall into the wrong and very dangerous hands."

SEVEN

hat's Nick Charles talking," said Myrna with an imperious sniff.

"I beg to differ," countered Powell. "Those were my very own pearls of wisdom. If that book gets into the wrong hands, there will be a lot of careers sinking below the horizon."

"This is turning out to be a terrible Christmas," said Myrna.

"Dash and I are having a perfectly lovely time," said Hellman. "We are, aren't we, Dash?"

"I *loathe* Christmas. But if you say so, Lily, we're having a perfectly lovely time. And if you want to know why I loathe Christmas, I shall tell all of you with great gusto, especially if there's more cognac in reserve." Griselda signaled a waiter to bring a bottle of cognac. "Christmas is the season of hypocrisy. I suppose it once was a time when mankind generally wanted peace on earth with good will toward all men. Very Charles Dickens and that tiresome child Tiny Tim — if he was standing next to me all hale and healthy, I'd take great pleasure in breaking both his legs."

"Spoken like a true curmudgeon," said Powell. "Griselda, are you appalled?"

"Not at all. I thrive on cynics. They're among my best customers. Mrs. Parker, Mr. Benchley, the Mankiewicz brothers, and the rest of the lot. I happen to like Christmas. I'm very sentimental. I also like Shirley Temple. Here's more brandy." The waiter refilled their snifters.

"Now these are *not* on the house," insisted Myrna. "We mustn't make pigs of ourselves and take advantage of a hostess who is brave enough to admit she likes Shirley Temple."

"What have you got against the kid?" asked Hammett, already on his way into his cups.

A startled Myrna said, "I've got nothing against her. She's charming and very gifted and I never speak ill of a fellow thespian. And I stand by my statement. This isn't a very nice Christmas what with the sword of Damocles hanging overhead and threatening the careers of so many nice people."

Added Hellman, "Whose only crime was getting horny every so often and going in search of artificial respiration. This town is absolutely unbelievable. It seduces and then it destroys what it has seduced."

"Don't be too unkind to this town," said Myrna. "It's the only town I've got."

"There, there, Minnie, don't go getting maudlin on us," said Powell consolingly. "Soon Christmas will have passed and we'll be facing paying income tax."

"Gee, but you're a fun bunch," said Hellman.

"And I haven't sent my Christmas cards," moaned Myrna. "Arthur is such a louse. I hope he drowns in a vat of imported French wine."

"If you miss him so much," said Powell, "why don't you phone him and tell him to come home?"

"He *is* home. I'm the one who isn't! He should be on his knees pleading with me to come back."

"I don't see Arthur as the pleading type, especially on his knees."

"They're very knobby knees," said Myrna.

Griselda interrupted. "He's alone."

"I don't give a damn if he is," said an angry Myrna.

"I'm referring to Doctor Carewe," said Griselda. "Fern's abandoned him. He looks very unhappy."

"Serves him right for turning me down. I seem to get turned down more often than a blanket." Myrna was staring across the room. "He's paying the check."

"They didn't eat," added Griselda.

"They each had a drink," said Powell.

"My God!" cried Hellman, "you sound like undercover agents!"

Said Powell, "I wish I had a recording of their conversation." He took a sip of cognac and then added, "Does anyone feel as uneasy as I do at this very moment?"

"I understand, Bill," said Myrna. "There's an awful lot to feel uneasy about."

"Brrrr," said Griselda. "I'm suddenly cold all over."

"Somebody must have walked over your grave," suggested Myrna.

"Well, if they did," said Griselda, "they chose the wrong grave. I don't own a little black book."

Claire Young sat alone in her living room in an easy chair, on her lap an unopened Bible. One hand covered the Bible as though she was swearing an oath. The other hand held a glass filled with bourbon and soda. On the end table at her side, a cigarette smoldered in a tray. Claire's hair was pulled back and tied with a ribbon. She wore pajamas and a negligee but sleep was the furthest thing from her mind. A sound at the front door brought her suddenly alert. She heard a key turning in the lock. She hurried to a bookshelf and replaced the Bible. Fern Arnold came into the room.

"Oh God, Fern, how you frightened me. I had visions of someone using a skeleton key."

"Who'd be dumb enough to use a skeleton key when a house is ablaze with light? I thought you had company. Lots of company. I tried to phone but I kept getting a busy signal." Her eye caught the phone. The receiver was off the hook. "You put the phone off the hook. Lots of crank calls?"

"Lots of reporters. A couple of Johns wanting to make sure I was out of business. I get a new unlisted number tomorrow. I'll have cards printed and mail them to our gentlemen callers."

Fern sat opposite Claire on the sofa, lighting a cigarette. "Gentlemen callers! That's a rich one."

Said Claire pragmatically, "They'll have to know where to get in touch."

"They could always come by and scratch at the door. How's for a drink?"

Claire held up her bourbon and soda. "I've already got one."

"It looks very watery." She took the glass from Claire as she headed for the bar.

"Where've you been? I tried to call you."

"Where are the smelling salts?"

Claire stared at her. "Don't you feel well?"

"I feel fine. It's you I'm considering." She was mixing two bourbon and sodas, the cigarette dangling from the edge of her mouth.

"Do I look as though I'm about to faint?" There was now an edge to Claire's voice.

"Don't get tetchy with me. I know it's no fun to be under fire. Well, hon, you should have thought it over more carefully before going public."

Claire folded her arms and said with a self-confident smile, "In the past three hours there have been five messengers bringing me envelopes."

Fern's eyes widened. "And does your cup runneth over as it says somewhere in the good book?"

"It's not yet an inundation, but it's a promising start."

"And it's nontaxable. Whee!" She carried the drinks back to Claire and retained what was a stronger one for herself. As she returned to the sofa, she asked, "You think it's safe to stay in the house?"

"No I don't. But I have to sit it out until I can make a move."

"Move where? Your doctors are here."

"Singular doctor as of now. Mitch Carewe."

"That's who I was with tonight." Claire looked like a startled rabbit. "That's why I've been thinking of smelling salts. I didn't want to see him but he was so damned persistent, I figured why the hell not. I met him at Griselda's Cage. We had a drink with a brief interruption by Bill Powell."

"One of the few nice ones in this town. Was he with Harlow?"

Fern told her about Powell's companions and then about Carewe's ardent insistence on his love for Claire. Claire commented succinctly, "Hogwash. He's after what a hell of a lot of other people would like to get their hands on, my little black book."

"Say, listen. Where do you keep it hidden?" Claire said nothing. "Does it exist?"

"It exists along with some heavy dictation I gave Amelia Hubbard."

"How heavy is heavy?" Fern was staring at Claire over the rim of her glass as she took a healthy swig.

"Heavy."

"Am I in it?"

"Yes, but I used a different name."

"I don't give a damn one way or another. Claire, I've been giving you and me and the business a lot of thought. I want to take over."

"It's nothing like running a bakery."

"I never ran a bakery so I can't make comparisons. I'll do a good job. I'll give you a fair cut. I know all the clients and I know most of them like me."

"Why shouldn't they? You always offered to pick up their dry cleaning."

Fern laughed and then said, "I think most of the girls would stick with me."

"Those who haven't already made other arrangements. The joy girls in this town move fast."

Fern said, "I'll give you a fair share of the take until after — " She caught herself.

Claire smiled. "Fern, my darling, sing no sad songs for me. Just always take care of the two out in Venice, should they need help. I'm doing my damnedest to see them well fixed. From the look of tonight's . . . shall we say, donations? . . . it looks very promising."

"Claire, I don't mind telling you, I'm afraid."

"Of what?"

"Of what could happen to you."

"Don't be silly, hon. Either way, it's a ticket to the boneyard." She sipped her drink and then said, "Everybody's listed in my address book, including the phony names they used. That goes for the girls. And when you talk to the girls, don't push them. If they don't want to be with you, then that's that. If you're doing real well by the girls who stick with you, then rely on them to spread the word. Whores love to brag. It gives them a feeling of self-esteem, like when I paired up Freda Groba, the Hungarian madwoman, with Albert Einstein."

"I remember him not being very happy with her."

"In the sack he was happy. But out of the sack, when she began to feed him *her* theory of relativity . . ." Claire rolled her eyes.

In a tidy bungalow in West Hollywood on a quiet residential street, the Hungarian whore sat before her bedroom dressing table mirror adjusting earrings. Behind her, a Hungarian violinist by the name of Lazlo Biro, in his thirties with hair that grew down to his shoulders, wearing an ill-fitting suit and what he hoped was a soulful expression, was worrying his violin with "When a Gypsy Makes His Violin Cry." Freda was unaffected by the schmaltzy musicianship, but Freda's friend Lucy Rockefeller sat on the bed, sniffling and dabbing at her eyes with a tissue. Rockefeller wasn't her real name, but she had adopted it because it made her feel rich. In New York City she had been known as Lucy Vanderbilt and during a brief sojourn in Chicago called herself Lucy Astor hyphen Hutton, but didn't do too well there because her madam wasn't a go-getter. It was in Hollywood that she found her true métier as a prostitute and was soon known as Juicy Lucy, not because she wept at the sound of cheap music but because she wept at the drop of a trouser. Her clients got used to her saluting their endowments and then pulling out a rosary and telling her beads what she would rarely tell anyone else. Lucy was a dedicated prostitute who harbored a secret desire to open a School for Prostitution where she would train young women in the fine art of whoring. She had once discussed this with Freda Groba, who had commented in her thick Hungarian accent, "So vot is to teach, dollink? Fawking is fawking, give or take an artistic embellishment. It is a school for men you should be thinking about, the pigs. They need to be taught manners and finesse and the fine art of making a whore feel like a lady instead of a service station."

Through her dressing table mirror, Freda could see Lucy's tear-stained face. Freda clucked her tongue and shook her head slowly from side to side. She would never go to a movie with Lucy because the young woman sobbed bitterly when the opening credits rolled, sobbing at the expectation of having her heart broken, especially if it was a Greta Garbo film. "Lucy, vot is with the tears? You have heard Lazlo play this melody dozens of times. Lazlo! Play something fonny!" Lazlo leapt atop the bed and began fiddling away with great enthusiasm at "The Flight of the Bumble Bee," with which he had placed third in a musical competition when his parents were touting him as a child prodigy.

Lucy said through her tears, "What's to become of us with Claire going out of business?"

"Ve'll do just fine," said Freda, with true Hungarian self-confidence.

"Do you suppose Fern might take over the business?" asked Lucy eagerly, her face streaked with mascara.

Freda thought for a moment. "You know, iz very good idea. Fern knows most of the ropes and vot she doesn't know, I will teach her." She thought again. "Maybe I teach her tricks handed down through the centuries by the Groba women. From mother to daughter and etcetera and etcetera until my mother handed the legacy on to me."

Lucy was awe-struck. "All them generations of hookers. I guess you're the end of the line, Freda?"

"And why so?" asked Freda with ruffled indignation. "I can have baby! I'm still young enough!"

"Supposing it's a boy," asked Lucy.

Freda's hands were outstretched. "So I teach boy!" Her eyes now sparkled as she said with pride, "Lots boy prostitutes all over the world, especially in Bangkok. Right here in Hollywood, you know how many male stars began by bartering their bodies?" She rattled off an impressive list, which was interspersed with an astonished "No!" from Lucy while Lazlo accompanied Freda with "Love Me or Leave Me." When Freda had completed her litany, there was a faraway look in her eyes and her face was a study.

"Freda?" asked Lucy. "What's that funny look on your face?"

"My face has fonny look?"

"What were you thinking about?"

"I was thinking about Claire's little black book." Freda stared at her image in the dressing table mirror. Telltale lines had not begun to appear around her eyes and her mouth. There were no liver spots on the back of her hands. How much time did she really have? Her efforts to become a rich man's darling in the three years since she had settled in Hollywood had so far been in vain. Short-term options were available, but if she was to be categorized as damaged goods she would do so on her own terms. She had invested her money well with tips from stockbroker and lawyer clients who admired her élan and her *joie de vivre,* not to say her devil-may-care attitude, an asset drummed into her by her mother, who was now a countess by marriage living in a town house in Vienna with an impressively rich husband. Freda suspected he was being fed death in small doses of strychnine provided by her mother's secret lover, a young chemist with ambitions to direct motion pictures.

"That little black book has got to be worth a king's ransom," said Lucy. "Have you ever seen it?"

"No," said Freda softly, "no, my dear. And I don't mind telling you, I would kill to get my hands on it."

Lucy moved forward on the bed. Lazlo was playing the melodramatic and overwrought "Ase's Death" as Lucy said, "You couldn't kill, Freda. Not you. You've got too good a sense of humor to be a murderer." Lucy caught her reflection with the mascara streaks, groaned, and went to the dressing table for some fresh tissues and some of Freda's cold cream. It then occurred to Lucy there had been no reaction from Freda to her statement. Lucy repeated, "You couldn't kill, could you?"

"Lucy, my dear friend, there is old Hungarian expression, 'There is a first time for everything.'" Their eyes met in the mirror and Lucy was frightened by what she saw. Then Freda smiled, and all seemed right with the world. "Come, my dollinks, or we'll be late for the orgy."

The next morning featured a hazy sun in a cloudy sky. Maidie Casson stood on the porch of her bungalow in Venice Beach and looked out at the Pacific Ocean, where dolphins were playing tag with each other. Maidie's house was separated from the ocean by Ocean Front Walk, miles of concrete on which abutted other bungalows and many bars and sleazy cafes. Ocean Front Walk was separated from the Pacific by a long stretch of beautiful sandy beach dotted with sun bathers and sun worshipers and a small army of male body builders, who were responsible for this area being known as Muscle Beach. The body builders struck poses and lifted friends on their shoulders or did handsprings while others exercised on the parallel bars and other gym paraphernalia provided by the thoughtful fathers of Venice Beach. Maidie looked wistfully at the beach boys, wishing she was thirty years younger when she would have been strong competition from the admiring girls calling encouragement to their boyfriends. She picked up the bottle of milk she had come out to collect and went inside where a table radio blared for a ten-year-old boy in a wheelchair listening to a popular children's program, *Let's Pretend,* which weekly dramatized a fairy tale.

"Sounds familiar, Elmer. What is it? 'Rapunzel'?"

"It's 'The Ugly Duckling.'" A series of quacks came from the radio. "Sounds pretty ugly. I'm tired of this kid stuff." He turned off the radio, deftly spun the wheelchair around, and pointed to a table on which was stacked a deck of cards. "Tell me about the future again, Aunt Maidie. Come on, tell me again.''

Telling futures was Maidie Casson's avocation. She had no future of her own to speak of and her past wasn't worth flaunting. The present was some kind of question mark, so Maidie lived from day to day expecting nothing, getting nothing, and so was never disappointed. She loved the boy in the wheelchair, her niece's son, and her niece paid her handsomely for the devotion. The boy was very little trouble. When not listening to the radio, a recent gift from his mother as the first of the many Christmas gifts he would receive, he read books voraciously, unless he was entertaining a secret desire to be a drummer in a jazz band. He knew that Chick Webb, the colored drummer who led his own orchestra, was a cripple but you couldn't tell from his performance on the radio. When next he saw his mother, he'd bring up the possibility of her buying him a set of drums. It didn't occur to him the noise might disturb Maidie and the neighbors, because like all lads his age, he was single-minded.

Maidie waved the young polio victim to the table, where she commenced shuffling a deck of cards. He had detoured to look out the window at the muscle boys he envied and then resumed his way to his aunt. "Cut the cards," ordered Aunt Maidie, which he did. She laid out five cards and studied them. "The ace of clubs and the eight and the ten. They're good luck." He'd heard it all before and loved it. Maidie was very dramatic with a beautifully expressive face. "Here it is again, the ten of diamonds, the money card." She laid out five more cards, "Well, hot damn, we're going to be on the move soon."

"Where to?"

"You know where to. I've told you often enough. Someplace that'll be good for your polio. Some place like maybe Palm Springs or farther out to Palm Desert and you'll have a swimming pool where we can exercise your legs and have you up and walking again, as good as new. You know, President Roosevelt goes to Warm Springs — you remember that's in Georgia — to exercise his legs while his mother Sara exercises her mouth. Tough old bird, Sara."

Elmer giggled.

"What's so funny all of a sudden?"

"You. You're a tough old bird."

"Oh yes? Well, I'm not so tough and I'm not *that* old."

"Will my mom come to live with us?"

"She'll visit as often as she can."

"I didn't say 'visit,' I said 'live with us.' "

"Maybe she will." The phone rang. Maidie placed the cards on the table and went to the phone. "Hello? Well, speak of the devil. Elmer and I were just talking about maybe moving to the desert and maybe you living with us."

At the other end of the phone Claire Young said, "No maybes about it. We'll be together . . ." She was about to say "for the rest of our lives" but found herself fighting tears.

"Claire? You all right, Claire?" Elmer had wheeled himself to Maidie's side and was looking up at her anxiously.

"I'm fine, Maidie. Let me talk to Elmer for a minute, and then you come back on."

"Here he is, honey, as anxious as ever."

Elmer took the phone and said eagerly, "Hey Mom, when you coming to see us?"

"How's my baby?" She was in the kitchen with Fern, who was staring glumly into a cup of black coffee. An awful lot of bourbon had been consumed the previous evening and Fern's head throbbed.

"I'm fine, Mom. Are we really going to move to the desert?"

"Do you want to live in the desert? It can be pretty lonely, you know."

"Maidie says it would be good for my legs. We'd have a pool where I can exercise. Don't you think that's a good idea?"

"I think it's a terrific idea." She wondered if any madam had staked out the desert territory but then scrubbed the idea. She wouldn't live long enough and she'd face problems transporting girls from L.A. "Sweetheart, let me talk to Maidie for a minute. It's something I don't want to forget."

Maidie took the phone and said, "Before you say another thing,

I want you to know he's perfectly fine. He's eating good and he loves the radio. *Jack Armstrong, the All-American Boy, Pepper Young's Family, Buck Rogers,* and I can't get enough of *Myrt and Marge* and *Eddie Cantor* — "

Claire finally interrupted. "Maidie, listen to me, I've got things to tell you . . . Maidie? Will you shut up?"

"Sure, sure. What's wrong. What's eating you?"

"Cancer, goddamn it," she shouted, "that's what's eating me!"

"Oh God," said Fern, lighting a cigarette, "did you have to hit her with it that way?"

E I G H T

$\mathcal{I}$n the downtown police precinct from which Herb Villon and Jim Mallory operated, the two detectives sat in Villon's office drinking coffee out of cardboard containers. Jim Mallory was reading aloud to Villon an item in gossip writer Jimmy Fidler's column. It was about Claire Young, and Fidler was wondering in print if Claire Young remembered a promising young actress of yesteryear by the name of Audrey Manners. Jim asked Villon, "You ever hear of this Audrey Manners? I don't remember any actress with that name."

Herb sat back in his swivel chair and contemplated a framed print on the opposite wall depicting a timeworn biblical scene of Noah's Ark at the Ararat landfall. "Audrey Manners was a stunner." His voice sounded as though it was coming from an echo chamber.

Jim lowered the paper and stared at Villon. "Did you know her?"

"I was in love with her."

Mallory folded the paper and placed it on Villon's desk. Intuition told him he was about to hear a very interesting piece of Villon's history. He wanted to savor the moment and then treasure it. In the eight years he'd been working with Villon, he was frequently frustrated by the man's reticence. He knew Villon had a mother and father because here he was sitting behind his desk, and Mallory was positive he hadn't sprung from the top of somebody's head as Topsy claimed in *Uncle Tom's Cabin*. He knew there was a sister in the Midwest whom he didn't particularly like and there was a brother in the armed forces from whom he rarely heard. He knew Hazel Dickson was his lover because when Hazel staked out a territory she trumpeted her triumph to the world.

"Yes?" said Mallory.

"Yes what?"

"You were in love with her."

"Didn't I say that?"

Mallory was waxing impatient. "Well, don't leave me hanging there!"

"What are you talking about?"

"Audrey Manners! You said you were in love with her." He indicated the newspaper. "Jimmy Fidler wants to know if Claire Young remembers her. And then you say you were in love with her. So then what happened?"

"You're whining."

"Sorry. Well come on, Herb, tell me about this Manners dame."

"She was no dame. She's a lady."

"What's become of her? Where is she now?"

Villon looked at his wristwatch. "Probably having breakfast."

"Are you in touch with her?"

"We talk on the phone from time to time. When she has a problem she can't deal with, I deal with it for her. Like the occasional police shakedown. When the mob tries to step in and threaten her. I'm the white knight galloping to her rescue."

"Claire Young? Claire Young was Audrey Manners?"

"One of Metro's baby stars." He sighed and sat forward, extrcating a cigarette from a pack on his desk and then lighting it.

"Now wait a minute! You said you'd never met Claire Young."

"That was for Hazel's benefit. Metaphorically speaking, when Audrey Manners died, Claire Young gave her a decent funeral.

There really wasn't an Audrey Manners. Audrey was created by the studio the way Billie Cassin became Joan Crawford, who was born Lucille LeSueur. Claire erased as much of Audrey as she could. When her secret benefactor set her up in business, Audrey was determined to start fresh. The man was a power at Metro then so he had all traces of Audrey Manners destroyed. Photographs, memos concerning her, all that crap, but judging from Fidler's column, it wasn't too thorough a job."

Jim said, "I don't think you can ever wipe somebody off the face of the earth entirely. Somewhere there are dedicated movie buffs who have Audrey Manners photos in their files."

"But they don't know she became Claire Young. She covered her tracks and has kept them covered."

"Until now. I wonder who gave Fidler the Audrey Manners tip?"

"Maybe he didn't need a tip. He's been around a long time. I suspect he's in the little black book along with every other male gossipmonger. You ever meet any of these guys at Claire's?"

"You only meet girls at Claire's. She sets appointments so that you don't run into anyone you know. She has an uncanny gift for subterfuge." A thought developed. "Would Hazel have known about Audrey Manners? Her nose for news makes Pinocchio's look like a pencil stub. She told us Fern Arnold gave her the exclusive on the black book and Claire's decision to close up shop."

Villon was out of the chair and pacing in circles around his desk and Jim Mallory. His hands were shoved deep into his trouser pockets and his brow was furrowed with trouble lines. "It's all too pat, Claire folding the business and letting the world know there's a little black book that could prove to be very troublesome."

"Or very profitable. Come on, Herb, be realistic. She may be an old buddy of yours but what she's doing sounds like a clever heist and blackmail is blackmail."

Villon sat on the desk looking down at Mallory. "I'll stand by my statement that Claire is a lady. I don't say ladies sometimes don't stoop to blackmail, because I've had to deal with a few in the past, but that's because their backs were against the wall. And if Claire's back is against the wall, I want to know why it's there and who helped put it there."

"What about this guy who helped set Claire up in business?"

"He's bye-bye forever. If it's finances that have her in trouble, I'm positive she has no one to turn to unless she was ever chummy with William Randolph Hearst but somehow I can't quite see that." He was thinking aloud. "It's like there's some sort of a shoot-out going on and Claire is deliberately moving into the line of fire."

"Anyway you look at it," said Mallory, "she's a clay pigeon."

"Damn it, for some reason, I think she wants to be one. I've got to find out."

Jim said, "You really care."

"Of course I care."

"You're still in love with her."

"Oh, for crying out loud!" Villon waved Jim's statement away with a toss of a hand. He took his jacket from the back of his swivel chair where it was always draped and headed out of the office, Mallory tagging in his wake. As they passed a row of holding cells, both suddenly stopped in their tracks. They heard someone playing a violin. The tune was "Play, Fiddle, Play." They had heard it often enough on the radio, especially the Sunday night show *The A.&P. Gypsies*.

"Lazlo," said Mallory.

"Is that a secret password?" asked Villon.

"It sounds like Lazlo. He plays violin exclusively for Freda Groba."

"Who is Freda Groba?"

Mallory cleared his throat. "She's a Hungarian whore. One of Claire's girls."

"I see. Am I to assume you have met Freda Groba?"

Mallory said staunchly, "I have met Freda Groba and have absolutely no regrets."

Villon said, "Her I've got to see." They followed the trail of the violin music as it grew louder and louder. They reached the cell in which Freda and Lazlo were incarcerated along with Lucy Rockefeller, who was emitting some heart-rending sobs.

"Freda," said Mallory, "I thought you were too clever to be pinched."

"I am always being pinched!" she said with a lavish smile. "Are you a gift from heaven? Look, Lucy, one of my favorite admirers." Lucy looked and now her body shook with heavier sobs.

"What's the matter with her?"

Freda asked, "You have never had the pleasure of Lucy Rockefeller?"

"She one of Claire's girls?" Villon was fascinated by the colloquy between whore and detective.

"An alumna. Lazlo," she said sharply, "I have had enough of music for the soul. Select another venue." Lazlo segued into "Home on the Range." "Dollink, could you perhaps be of some help? After all, we were leaving the orgy when the cops raided. Apparently they were late as they had trouble finding the house, it is so deep in the Hollywood Hills. It's not as though they found us *in flagrente delicious*. We were getting into my car when they came up the driveway."

"Where's the rest of the orgy?" asked Villon.

Lucy said between sobs, "They got sprung already."

"I left word with Claire's attorney, Ronald Derwitt, but something has delayed him." Freda said to Mallory, "But what are you doing here? Why are you in police station?"

Jim wished he could wipe the smirk off Villon's face. "I work here."

"You vork here? What kind of vork you do here?"

"I'm a detective."

"A detective? I have been fawked by a detective?" She shrieked with laughter. "Oh oh oh, when I write Mama and tell her, she will dine off the story for weeks." She shrieked with laughter again. Lucy's sobs had abated and Lazlo was inspired to play "Goodie Goodie." Freda's hand reached out to Mallory between the bars. "My good friend Irving Smith, can't you help us?"

Villon stared at Mallory and guffawed. "Irving Smith!"

Mallory was perspiring. "Well, you didn't expect me to give her my real name, did you?"

"Vy you no tell me you are detective?" demanded Freda.

"It might have given you a heart attack!"

"Aha! A considerate detective!" She thought for a moment. "Of course. You are a friend of Claire's. A, how they call it, a payoff. That is right?"

"That is wrong," countered Mallory. "I got a discount."

"Is also good but in a small way. Please," she implored the detectives, "perhaps they have set bail. You vould ask them to consider my i.o.u.?"

Villon said to Mallory. "Go to the desk and get a release order for these three. Whoever's there, tell them I said so in case he tries to give you an argument." Mallory was wiping his forehead with a handkerchief as he hurried off.

Freda said to Villon, "I am forever in your debt. We three are forever in your debt. Ask of us anything. Ask anything, it will be yours."

"Okay, tell the fiddler to play 'Body and Soul.' It's one of my favorites."

Amelia Hubbard's apartment in West Hollywood was tidy though a bit on the shabby side. She had been taking dictation from Claire for over an hour, Claire having come to her because Amelia's car wouldn't start that morning. It was a 1929 Ford two-seater with a rumble seat and Claire advised her to donate it to the Smithsonian.

"This is real hot stuff, Claire. Real hot stuff. Is that true about Victor McLaglen and Dolores Del Rio?"

"Every word of it."

"Oh boy, if this ever gets published, they ain't gonna like it." Claire dictated some more and Amelia let out a sudden yelp, sounding like a puppy whose tail had been stepped on.

"What's wrong?" asked Claire.

"Not H. B. Warner! He couldn't have been a regular at them orgies of Lionel Atwill's."

"Amelia, if I say he was there, he was *there.*"

Amelia was crushed. "But he was in *The King of Kings.*"

"So?"

Amelia said reverentially, "He played Jesus Christ."

"Oh, that explains it," said Claire. "He always asked if it was okay if he wore a crown of thorns. That picture must have unhinged him." Amelia looked chagrined. Claire asked, "Look, honey, if you're not up to any more of this, I'll get somebody else."

"Hell no!" protested Amelia, "it's an education!"

"I'm tired. Let's quit. I was at my lawyer's doing my will."

"Is it still Ronald Derwitt?"

"It's been Ronald from the time I started the business. He was bequeathed to me by an old friend at Metro. If there's ever any trouble and I'm not around, get in touch with him."

"What kind of trouble could there be?"

"Just trouble, that's all. Just trouble. You know this town. You've been around it long enough. You know the kind of mischief they can brew here."

Amelia held up her stenographer's pad. "Like the kind you're brewing?"

"That isn't mischief," said Claire. "That's the God's honest truth." She opened her handbag, retrieved a small envelope, and handed it to Amelia. "Here, honey. This should do you some good for a while."

Amelia took the envelope, opened it, and extracted a check, and as she stared at the figure her eyes widened. "Gee, Claire, this is more than I quoted."

"There's more where that came from. Lots more. You're worth every penny."

Amelia closed the stenographic pad and placed it on an end table at her side. "Good thing I'm not a prude or I'd burn this thing."

"You better not or I'll come back and haunt you."

Amelia looked confused. "What do you mean?"

Claire covered the slip. "Have you forgotten one of my favorite threats? Watch out or after I'm dead I'll come back and haunt you."

Amelia said, "I think what you're telling me is that you think somewhere out there there's a bullet with your name on it."

"Why a bullet? Why not a knife or poison or a speeding car?"

Amelia took Claire's hand and squeezed it. "You're not afraid. You act as though you don't give a damn."

"Enough of melodrama. Keep these pages stashed in a safe place. There are those who know I use you as a secretary."

"So?"

"There are those who might suspect I'm spilling the beans. There are those who don't want the beans spilled."

Amelia stood up and took a dramatic pose, with arms outstretched. "I shall guard these pages with my life."

"Fine. And while we're on the subject of your life, get yourself a new car. That jalopy of yours is a terminal case."

"What's wrong?" Claire said nothing. She couldn't. She was choked up. "You look like you're going to cry."

"It's because I'm tired. Yesterday, today, it's catching up with me."

"You want a drink? I've got some Manischewitz wine. A gift from an old admirer. My mother."

"No wine. No nothing. I'm going home and lie down."

"Why do I feel you need someone to look after you?"

Claire managed a smile. "Fern is looking after me. She's at home waiting for me."

"Good old Fern. Old faithful. True blue and reliable."

"Good old Fern and good old Amelia." She patted Amelia's cheek. "I'll call you in the morning." She blew her a kiss and was out the door. Amelia stood staring at the door Claire shut behind her.

You better not or I'll come back and haunt you.

The dictation at a feverish pace. The little black book. Folding the business. *Haunt you.*

Dear God, she said to herself, it can't be. It can't be. She sat down and stared at the stenographic pad. She opened the pad and began reading her shorthand notations. Some of it was funny. Some of it was sad. Claire dictated in a very matter-of-fact voice. It wasn't as though she was speaking startling revelations. She was like an accountant giving statistics. Claire had to know it was incendiary. Claire had to know there were those who would kill to suppress the book. And there was someone who might be determined to kill Claire.

Amelia suppressed a shudder. Claire wants to be killed. That's got to be it. Claire wants to be killed.

You better not or I'll come back and haunt you.

She found the bottle of wine and poured herself a glassful. She lit a cigarette. She stared at the stenographic pad she had put back on the table and then looked at the closet door behind which on the upper shelf she had placed yesterday's typewritten pages.

Claire's dying. Amelia had to know for sure. She had to know. She stared at her typewriter and at the sheet of paper onto which she had been transposing dictation when Claire arrived. She crossed to the phone and dialed Information. She asked for Dr. Mitchell Carewe's number. She jotted it down. Now she waited for the courage to phone him.

N I N E

$\mathcal{Y}$ou know what this case lacks," William Powell said to Myrna Loy at about the time Claire was giving Amelia dictation, "it lacks a corpse."

"Good heavens. How dare they deprive us of a corpse." Myrna was staring at herself in a compact mirror while waiting for Regan to deliver their club sandwiches. Each had a very dry gin martini in front of them. Powell lit a cigarette after which he nodded at several colleagues who were waving at him. One colleague was pointing a finger at Myrna indicating he wanted to wave at her too.

"Myrna?"

"What?"

"Franchot Tone would like to wave at you."

"Why?"

"I don't know. I suppose he's partial to waving."

Myrna said while still engrossed with her reflection, "It's Walter Pidgeon who's partial to waving. Once on the set he nodded off but his hand kept moving."

Powell observed, "I think Franchot is beginning to feel snubbed."

"We can't have Franchot thinking that. Heaven forbid. He might complain to his wife and she might get Mr. Mayer to put me on suspension."

"Miss Crawford wouldn't do that to you."

"Why not? She elbowed me out of *Forsaking All Others* and got the part for herself. There!" She snapped the compact shut and sought Franchot Tone. She found him and waved. "Oh good. He's smiling. He does have an enchanting smile, don't you think?"

"That depends on one's definition of an enchanting smile. Minnie Mouse has an enchanting smile."

"I'm in complete accord on that." She sipped her drink and tossed her head haughtily. "You're forgetting Jean."

"I could never forget Jean." He stared at his drink. " I wish they'd stop putting these oversize olives in my drink. They occupy so much space. Didn't we ask for lemon twists? The world's against us."

"Did you breakfast with Baby this morning?", asked Myrna, ignoring the olives.

"No, she didn't spend the night. As a matter of fact, I dined with Jean and her mother this morning."

"You breakfasted with Jean and her mother."

"Are you trying to tell me that when one eats breakfast one is not dining?"

Myrna thought it over while toying with the stem of her martini glass. Finally she spoke. "One is dining when one eats dinner. Just as one lunches when one is eating lunch, and I hope our sandwiches will soon materialize. And when one is at breakfast, one breakfasts. Breakfast meaning to break a fast, having slept all night and therefore eaten nothing."

"That's not entirely true. Some people awaken in the middle of the night and raid the refrigerator."

"They won't find anything worth raiding in mine."

Powell said as he folded his arms, "I'm considering wringing your neck."

"Why don't you consider wringing Franchot's neck." She could see the actor's reflection in the wall mirror behind Powell. "He's waving again."

"Not at us. He's waving at Virginia Bruce. She's at the next table. Oh now she's smiling at us. Smile, Myrna. She was with us in *The Great Ziegfeld.*"

Myrna turned her head and smiled and then said to Powell, "I'm getting a bit dizzy what with all this waving and smiling. Now, let's get back to Jean and her mother. Did you convince Mama Jean that Baby looks as though she needs a doctor?"

"No, I'm afraid I didn't. We found a compromise. She's taking Baby to a health spa on Catalina."

"Well, that's a step in the right direction." Regan arrived with their sandwiches as Myrna said, "You're right, Bill. We need a corpse." Regan almost dropped their plates. "Steady, dear."

Powell asked Regan, "Any new nerve-shattering tips for us today?"

"Yeah. Your ex is shacking up with Clark Gable."

"No!" He exchanged a glance with Myrna, who had busied herself scaling down her club sandwich from three slices of bread to two. "Did you hear that, Mrs. Hornblow?"

"Frequently this week. From my hairdresser, my manicurist, the wardrobe mistress, and a desk clerk at the Chateau Marmont, who voiced a very fervent disapproval. He wants Clark for himself."

"The very idea, the hussy."

Regan asked, "You want another round of drinks?"

Myrna asked for tea with lemon. Powell opted for black coffee. He told Myrna, "Have to have my wits about me. I'm being interviewed by Hazel Dickson."

"Not really."

"The one and only." Regan departed, wondering who was the elderly lady Franchot Tone was waving at on the opposite side of the room.

"Clutch opportunity by the throat," said Myrna. "See what you can get out of her."

"About what?"

"About what? Why, Claire Young of course. That might lead us to a corpse."

Powell leaned forward conspiratorially. "Frankly, my dear Myrna, I think Claire is our most likely candidate for a corpse."

"Hush!" She looked about with apprehension. "Lower your voice. You might incriminate yourself."

"How?"

"Well, supposing Claire is found murdered and you've been heard saying she's the most likely candidate for a corpse."

"The only one close enough to have heard is Virginia Bruce and she's still busy smiling, and heaven help me, Franchot's forgotten we already waved back and forth because he's waving again. Either that or he's doing semaphors."

Myrna said forthrightly, "He's had my last wave. I'm not waving again. I don't believe in overdoing a thing."

"I didn't sleep too well last night."

"You should have heated up some milk."

"I wasn't hungry, I was sleepy." He wasn't enjoying his sandwich. It was too thick, wet, and unmaneuverable. Myrna was doing fine with hers thanks to her having excised the third slice of bread. "Once it became obvious to me that I wasn't welcome in the arms of Morpheus, I got out of bed, put on my robe and went to the study where I poured myself a large highball." Myrna nodded by way of tacit understanding. "I sat in my favorite chair and gave Baby some thought and when there was soon very little more to think about, I centered my attention on Claire Young. You know, Myrna, although I do think she's the most likely candidate for a corpse, I think she's safe as long as the book remains hidden."

Myrna gave it some thought. "You might have a point there. First get your hands on the book, and then destroy it and her so she can't reveal the contents of the book."

Regan served the tea and the coffee. "Anything else? Dessert?"

Myrna asked, "Is there coconut cream pie?"

"There sure is," said Regan, sounding like a cheerleader.

"Well, don't you dare bring me any," said Myrna sternly.

"Me either," said Powell, "I don't like gooey desserts, thank you, Regan."

Regan left them, wondering if the actors at other studios were as nuts as those at M.G.M.

"You were saying?" Powell asked Myrna.

"Umm, oh yes. Find the book, destroy it and murder Claire. Dear God, is that me speaking? It sounds so awful! So cold-blooded!"

"You must face the reality of murder, the way we did the *Thin Man* murders. They too were awful and coldblooded."

"But those were movies. About as removed from reality as Louis B. Mayer."

"Franchot is waving at him. And Virginia is smiling at him. Their option renewals must be coming up and murder is murder whether in fact or fiction. Mark my words. Someone is going to be murdered."

"You're so sure of yourself," Myrna said.

"The set-up is perfect. There's a madam with a little black book, the contents of which could destroy a lot of careers. And I'll venture the guess that a large percentage of the names therein mentioned are emotionally unstable and will murder to protect their somewhat shaky reputations."

"Including you?"

"I don't have to. I've been reassured that my career is safe."

"Reassured by Louis B. Mayer? You trust him?"

"I have to trust him. He's all I've got. You think if all this gets too hot, he'll dump me?"

"He tried to dump me last year when I went on strike. He had me on suspension without salary for months. Arthur almost didn't marry me because I wasn't collecting a salary. Oh, the hell with Mayer and the hell with Arthur, let's talk about real people. You got any connections with the police?"

"Why? Do you think I might need them?"

"Well, it's always handy to have a policeman in your back pocket. Say, wait a minute. We had a dick on *Penthouse.*"

Powell was reaching for his cup of coffee but instead cocked his head to one side. "A 'dick?' "

"Well, isn't that what they call detectives?"

"Yes they do, but coming from you it sounds like a language from another world. A 'dick' indeed!"

"Stop trying to be superior. We had this officer on the movie. Now let me think. What was his name? Hmmm. It was something very poetic."

"Browning?" suggested Powell.

"No. That doesn't ring a bell."

"It did for Elizabeth Barrett."

"That's another part I was after. So was Marion Davies."

"Heavens."

"But Miss Shearer got it, as you well know."

"Joyce Kilmer?"

"You're not even warm."

Powell made a mock bow and said, *"Pardonnez-moi."*

"That's it!"

"That's what?"

"French! Villon! François Villon!"

"François Villon worked on *Penthouse*?"

Myrna was losing patience with him. "Of course not François Villon, but it was somebody Villon. Very attractive man too." And then came the dawn. "Say wait a minute! Hazel Dickson was his girlfriend."

"Our Hazel do sure get around." He smiled. "Could it possibly be Herb Villon?"

Myrna smiled. "Oh Bill, bless your heart."

"I met Herb Villon. When Carole and I had that unpleasant Russ Columbo experience."

"Oh yes. I forgot they were a romance after you two divorced."

"It wasn't much of a romance. It was his boyfriend who shot him."

"But it said in the papers it was accidental. They were examining a gun when it accidentally went off and killed Columbo. He had such a beautiful voice."

"The funeral was nice too."

"You were there?"

"I escorted Carole. She was very broken up, about as broken up as Carole can ever get."

"Don't be mean."

"I'm not telling you anything I haven't told her. She liked Columbo. She liked his boyfriend too. Underneath that wacky exterior of Miss Lombard's there beats the heart of a dedicated romantic. I hope she's happy with Gable."

"He's so dumb."

"Why, Mrs. Hornblow!"

"I'm not telling you anything that you and everyone who knows him isn't already aware of. He's a dear man and he's dumb. Let's go back to the detective."

"Where'd we leave him?"

Regan was back freshening their cups of tea and coffee.

"I presume we left him when he was investigating Columbo's so-called accidental shooting."

"You two are so blood thirsty what with needing a corpse and an accidental shooting!" Regan was appropriately bewildered.

Powell said, "We're just rehearsing dialogue for our next Nick and Nora Charles adventure, *The Thin Man Gains Weight*."

Regan stalked away but paused in her flight to see who Franchot Tone was waving at this time.

Myrna said, "So he was investigating the shooting and you were a great help to him."

"No I wasn't. I wasn't much help at all. Luckily for Carole, at the time of the shooting we were at her lawyer's signing papers and trading filthy jokes. You know, of course, Carole dotes on filthy jokes."

"I don't know that at all. She's always on her best behavior when I'm with her, which isn't very often."

"I was Carole's alibi."

"Why did she need an alibi? The shooting was accidental."

"How do you know?"

"You said so."

"What I said was hearsay and it wouldn't stand up in a court of law. My dear Myrna, the way Metro covered up Paul Bern's murder when Baby was married to him, Paramount engineered a cover-up of Columbo's killing to protect one of their very valuable properties, namely, Miss Carole Lombard."

"Are you telling me the gun didn't go off accidentally?"

"You look so disappointed. It was quite obvious the boyfriend in a jealous rage plugged him and thatta, as they say, was thatta. *Un crime passionel,* as the French would say, which brings us back to Mr. Villon. Now how do you expect a detective to help us? We are in no way involved in the crime that has yet to be committed and if it is committed we don't want to be anywhere near it."

"I'm sure Villon is well aware of what's going on with Claire and the little black book."

"Well, if he's still Hazel Dickson's boyfriend, he damn well ought to be."

"And I'll bet he's been in on some of those orgies."

"What? As a participant? Shameful, Mrs. Hornblow, shameful."

"You know what I mean! He led the raids."

"I doubt it. He's an investigative detective. They don't lead raids. They're not all that physical. They look for clues and do a lot of thinking about who might have perpetrated the crime."

"Bill, I find this all very frustrating."

"In the meantime, I'll toss you for the check."

"Oh no you won't. We'll go dutch the way we always do. There's Regan." She signaled Regan for the check and then rummaged in her handbag for her wallet. Powell had his wallet on the table. Regan handed him the check.

As he studied the check, Powell said, "I suggest we go to my dressing room and wait for Hazel Dickson to arrive." He looked at his wristwatch. "There's still plenty of time before she'll get here. Oh goody gumdrops. Perhaps I'll attempt to rape you."

Regan leaned against the table to steady herself.

Myrna was concerned. "Regan? Do you feel faint?"

"I don't know what I feel. First a corpse, then an accidental shooting, and now rape . . ."

Powell smiled and said, "We are a bit eclectic, aren't we?"

"If that means you're off your rockers, then you certainly are." She took the check and the cash and hurried off to the cashier.

Myrna asked, "Why do I think this innocent lunch of ours might show up in somebody's column? She is a spy, you know."

"And undoubtedly regrets she has but one studio to give for her country. What a lousy sandwich. Wipe that peculiar look off your face, Mrs. Hornblow. It's giving me the heebie-jeebies."

"I keep thinking of Claire Young," Myrna said resolutely. "Madam or no madam, blackmailer or no blackmailer, whatever she is or isn't, she's much too young to die."

TEN

Hazel Dickson had spent the morning having her hair done by Mr. Eleanor in his beauty parlor on Fairfax Avenue, just off Wilshire Boulevard. It was convenient to Hollywood's celebrated Farmers Market, where many of the stars shopped and Hazel frequently picked up some tips while doing her shopping. She had a legion of spies there among the produce vendors and their loyalty couldn't be faulted. Today she skipped the Farmers Market because there was just time to beard her favorite lion in his den, Villon in his precinct downtown. That would give her plenty of time to get to Metro in Culver City and her interview with William Powell commissioned by a magazine in Denmark. She kept reappraising herself in the rear-view mirror of her car and wasn't sure she liked what she saw. Mr. Eleanor had had a battle with his latest lover, a truck driver who was away on the road several times a week hauling gasoline for Texaco and he was still unnerved by the ordeal when working on Hazel. His hands shook and Hazel had a vision of herself emerging as the Bride of Frankenstein. Under the circumstances, she thought of suggesting he turn her over to his very capable assistant, Mr. Esmeralda, but once she was seated after having her hair washed, Mr. Eleanor began spouting the gossip he had picked up since he had last worked on her and much of it was choice. As he spouted away, Hazel silently admired the Christmas decorations and wondered what Villon was giving her.

Hazel inspected herself again in the rear-view mirror and questioned the permanency of the permanent wave. She was turning into the precinct's parking lot when she espied Villon and Jim Mallory emerging from the building and heading toward their unmarked police car. She bore down on her horn and then stopped the car and rolled down her window. "You heading for lunch? I'll join you."

"We're not heading for lunch. What did you do to your hair?"

Hazel panicked. "What's wrong? I just had it done!"

Villon consulted with Mallory. "Don't you think her hair's a little too red?"

Mallory squinted at Hazel's hair and then at her face and commented, "It doesn't match her eyebrows. They're black."

Hazel fumed, "Who ever heard of anybody with red eyebrows?"

Villon asked Mallory, "Didn't I read somewhere Captain Bluebeard had red eyebrows? Bushy red eyebrows?"

Mallory said to Villon, "You only read newspapers and coroner's reports. I never saw you crack a book."

"You're a big help."

Hazel's eyes darted from one man to the other. "You're pulling my leg."

"Never in broad daylight," said Villon. "What are you doing here?"

"I had a couple of hours to kill before an appointment with Bill Powell at Metro so I decided to drive here and see if you had any dirt for me."

Mallory asked Villon under his breath, "The orgy at Atwill's?"

Villon cautioned him, "She reads lips."

"Another orgy at Atwill's?" asked Hazel.

"You getting bored with them?" asked Villon.

"Everybody's getting bored with them. They have to be used as blind items because the columnists don't dare name names. Anybody unusual caught?"

"Baby LeRoy." Villon conjured up the erstwhile child actor from his long-dormant subconscious and wondered what had become of him. He could only be seven or eight years old, Villon figured, though in this town it could be considered an awkward age.

Hazel's eyes were narrowed into slits. "That's not funny. Where are you off to now?"

"I suppose if I don't tell you, you'll tail us anyway."

"Right on the nose."

"Claire Young's."

Hazel brightened. "Oh, is she back in business? That was a short retirement."

"I felt like having a talk with her."

"Why don't you phone her?"

"I did. She wasn't in but Fern Arnold was. She expected Claire back shortly, and by the time we get there, she ought to be there."

"I'm suspicious," said Hazel.

"That's a chronic condition with you."

"What's up, Herb? Has Claire had some death threats? Come on, out with it."

Herb Villon was losing patience with both the woman and the color of her hair. "I'm nursing a premonition." Hazel waited. "There's nothing else."

"I think there is," said Hazel. "Did you ever know an actress obscure in the annals of Hollywood history named Audrey Manners?"

Jim Mallory piped up, "Didn't I read her name in Jimmy Fidler's column today?"

"Either that or it was read to you. Herb? Did you ever hear of Audrey Manners?" Hazel had gotten out of the car and stood facing Villon. "I'll jog your memory. Maybe it'll help you. About twelve years ago she was under contract at Metro. She got into trouble with a producer whose wife blew the whistle on him and got Louis B. to drop the actress and blacklist her in the industry so no one else would hire her. Very nasty of him but what the hell, you know how nasty these big shots can get when they've got little else to do."

"Hazel, you're giving yourself a headache I don't think you want."

"Claire Young was thrown out of Metro and blacklisted," said Hazel. "I knew there was a story there someplace. I kept the idea in the back of my head until Fern Arnold gave me the fresh scoop on Claire. So I decided to do some poking around."

"Where did you do your poking?"

"In your apartment the other morning when you disappeared without waking me and kissing me goodbye."

"I was in a hurry."

"I was poking around in your desk for some writing paper. In the bottom drawer I found some pictures of some women. I figured you had a right to your personal gallery of old conquests."

"Mighty generous of you."

"They were all snapshots except one. It was a professional photo. The girl was very pretty. She looked familiar. On the back of the photo was the M.G.M. stamp and her name, Audrey Manners. I studied the picture for a long time, but I wasn't sure who it reminded me of. Then when Fern phoned me the scoop on Claire Young, something clicked."

Jim Mallory was feeling uncomfortable but wasn't quite sure why. Possibly the look on Herb Villon's face. It wasn't a pleasant look.

Hazel continued. "I'd been to Claire's. Fern took me there once after I promised not to write about it. That photo of Audrey Manners nagged at me, and you know what I'm like when something nags at me."

"Tenacious," said Villon. Mallory winced. Villon had spat the word.

Hazel wasn't fazed. The rare time she had been fazed was when Mae West invited her to tea and actually served tea. "So I went to one of the stores on Hollywood Boulevard who deal in movie nostalgia . . ."

The store was called Movie Memories and the young man behind the counter who had been sorting a stack of movie stills greeted her with a friendly smile. He wore a green eyeshade such as those fancied by croupiers in the films he had seen and when he smiled his teeth almost matched the color of the eyeshade.

"Can I help you?" he asked through his nose.

"You've helped me before. Perhaps you can help me again. As I recall, your studio photo file goes a long ways back."

"I've got one of the best in town. Say, now I remember you. You're the lady who offered me money if I had any tips for you. Did I ever give you any?"

"No, you didn't."

"Shame on me." He smiled and Hazel wished he wouldn't. "The only gossip I know is what I read in the columns, and I don't read those too often. I don't have the time."

"Are your pictures filed according to studio?"

"And cross-indexed. I do a lot of mail orders."

"There was an actress at Metro back in the twenties. Very young and very pretty."

"They all were. Who you looking for?"

"Her name is Audrey Manners."

He placed an index finger against a cheek and gave Audrey Manners some heavy thought. "Metro's in the back." He led Hazel down a row of shelves stacked with magazines, photographs, and an imposing serendipity of movie memorabilia. Hazel heard some employees chattering away interspersed with an occasional squeal of discovery. "Oh what a gorgeous picture of Natalie Moorhead!" "Say, don't Myrna Kennedy look real dishy here?" "Well, whaddya know, Ronald Colman without his mustache. And all along I thought he was born with it." etcetera.

At the back of the store, there was a long row of filing cabinets. "I keep the more obscure artistes in these cabinets. The ones for whom there isn't much call." He walked slowly reading the labels on each cabinet drawer, Hazel patiently following him. He suddenly stopped and asked her, "Is she still alive?"

"She must be. She's probably in her early thirties."

"So? She could have been crushed to death in a car smash-up. You know how they drive in this town. Sweet Mary Magdalene, I got rear-ended last weekend and could have sworn I heard Gabriel blowing his horn. It was a street musician, thank God." He slapped a fist on a cabinet that was ringed with black tape. "This is the land of the dead. Exclusively photos of those who have gone to their reward. Poor darlings. I've got everybody here. Dorothy Dell, Barbara LaMarr, Wallace Reid, Lilyan Tashman, Lowell Sherman, Bobby Harron. I've got some dirty ones of him, care to look?"

"No thanks."

"Very wise. They're positively nauseating. Ah, here we are." He read the label on the drawer: 'M.G.M. The Twenties. Ingenues.' " He asked Hazel, "Am I right in assuming she was an ingenue?" Hazel assured him he was. He pulled out the drawer and began riffling the photos. While flashing another unappetizing smile, he said, "Well, aren't you the lucky one. You must be an Aries." Hazel didn't confirm or deny, she was too anxious for a look at the photo he'd found. He pulled it out. *"Voila!* Audrey Manners. My, she was sweet."

The tableau of Hazel confronting Villon and Mallory in the parking lot needed regrouping. It was as though the three were frozen in position with Mallory wishing he was invisible. He and Villon realized that Hazel had dropped by accidentally on purpose. From the moment she found the Audrey Manners photograph in Villon's desk drawer, Villon realized she was being eaten up by a deadly combination of curiosity and jealousy.

"That was a fine piece of detective work, Hazel. I'd be jealous except as you know, I never envy anyone. And you didn't drop by here to see if I had any items for you."

"You said you'd never met Claire Young."

"I knew Audrey Manners."

"They're the same person!"

"It's one of those rare moments when you're not on my wave length. I knew Audrey Manners before she became Claire Young. I only know Audrey Manners. I repeat, I've never met Claire Young. I'm on my way to meet Claire Young now, assuming she'll be home by the time I get there." His tone softened. "Come on, Hazel. The past is dead. Let it rest in peace. If you've got the time before you have to meet Powell, tag along with us. It's on the way to the Metro studios. Or at least the golden retriever here" — he indicated Mallory with his head — "says it is." He sighed and said, "Hazel, you're pouting. The pout doesn't go with your new hairdo." He started for the unmarked car followed by Mallory, who flashed Hazel a wink. Hazel got back into her car, muttering under her breath.

"I'll kill that son of a bitch one of these days, so help me I'll kill him." She switched on the ignition and continued muttering. " 'I only know Audrey Manners . . . I've never met Claire Young.' Who does he think he's kidding? Audrey Manners is Claire Young and Claire Young was Audrey Manners. If you knew her under one name then you still know her even if she's changed it." She beeped angrily at a boy on a bicycle who was pedaling at a reckless speed. Villon thought she was beeping for his attention and beeped back by way of reassuring her. In his rear-view mirror he saw the menace on the bicycle. He slowed down so the boy could come abreast of him and then flashed his badge. The boy got the message and swerved sharply to the left into a side street. Through the rear-view mirror he saw Hazel bending over the wheel of her car as though she was competing in the Indy 500.

Villon said to Mallory, "Hazel's muttering. She's still mad at me."

"You've been talking to yourself."

"It's the only time I get smart answers."

"You want to talk about Audrey Manners?"

Villon ignored the question for the moment. "Damn Hazel! We've been together seven, eight years now and she still can't read me. Those photos she found in my desk drawer! She knows I know she snoops through my things when she's alone in the apartment. If I left those photos so accessible, she should know they mean nothing to me, they're unimportant."

Mallory stared ahead through the windshield and repeated his earlier question. "You want to talk about Audrey Manners?"

Villon growled, "Your needle's stuck."

"You're always pumping me about my girlfriends."

"You like me to pump you about your girlfriends."

"It isn't a matter of like or dislike. I consider you my best friend, Herb, and it pleases me you're interested in what's going on in my life, which usually isn't very much. Make a sharp right here." Villon followed instructions. The sudden turn caught Hazel unawares and she almost shot past the street Villon had turned into.

"Hazel's cursing," said Villon with a grin as he looked in his rear-view mirror.

Mallory was more interested in friendship than he was in Hazel. "It was pretty obvious you didn't like Reba."

"Reba? I don't remember any Reba."

"The salesgirl at Bullock's."

Villon searched his memory for Reba but she remained elusive. "I don't remember any Reba."

"Heliotrope."

"Oh my God. That one. That sickening scent she wore. Heliotrope. You finally get rid of her?"

"Three years ago."

"That long ago? My, how time flies. So, best friend, who're you mixed up with now?"

"I'll tell you if you promise not to laugh."

"I promise."

"She's a waitress. I've taken her dancing a couple of times. She doesn't mind dancing even though she's on her feet nine hours a day."

"Since when did you learn how to dance?"

"I haven't, but it doesn't seem to bother Regan."

"Who's Regan?"

"My waitress."

"Her name is Regan?"

"She works at Metro. In the executive dining room. She knows all the stars intimately and calls them by their first names."

"Even Garbo?"

"Garbo eats in her dressing room. She brings her lunch from home in a brown bag. She's very thrifty."

Villon said, "I don't believe she calls them by their first names."

"I think you're right."

"She probably calls them 'honey' or 'sweetie' or 'dearie' and aren't we there yet?"

"About another half mile."

Hazel was now muttering about Villon's poky driving. He was averaging thirty-five miles an hour and she was considering passing him and zooming on to Claire Young's. She knew the way. She'd been there before. *Audrey Manners.* Hazel was no longer tempted to pass the detectives. Audrey Manners had taken up residence again in her mind. They were practically old buddies. Hazel had been seriously entertaining Audrey ever since she found the still in Villon's desk drawer. She would have passed it off as unimportant because if it was lying around where Hazel could easily find it then it meant very little to him, if anything. But this was different. She had tracked Audrey to Claire like a bloodhound on the scent of an escaped convict. Even Herb had complimented her fine detective work. Neither one of them mentioned Jimmy Fidler wondering in his column today if Claire Young remembered an actress named Audrey Manners. She hadn't spilled the beans to Fidler, she had just asked him as a favor to use the query. She knew Fidler would soon ask her what it was all about, because she had a premonition something even bigger then the hidden black book was in the offing and Hazel's premonitions were notorious for their infallibility. She wondered who at Metro had been laying Audrey. Mayer? Always a possibility and rarely a dark horse. Who had bankrolled Audrey when she decided to change her name to Claire Young, throw caution to the winds, and go into high-class prostitution with the eagerness and verve of those who change their religions? If Louis B. Mayer found out his identity he'd have either finished him off for good in the business or demanded a season's pass. No, it wasn't safe to let any information fall into Mayer's hands that could serve as a threat to one's career. Ahead through the windshield she saw Herb Villon pulling into Claire Young's driveway. There was one car parked there and Hazel recognized it as Fern Arnold's. Claire had not yet come home.

Villon said to Mallory, "Modest little place by Hollywood standards."

"Claire doesn't go in for ostentation. She's always kept a low profile. I don't think she's home yet."

"Whose car is this?" asked Villon as he switched off the ignition.

"It's Fern Arnold's." Mallory got out of the car and waved at Hazel as she pulled in behind them.

Hazel said, after she got out of her car and slammed the door shut with such ferocity that both men winced, "Herb Villon, you are a menace. You are the worst driver ever. You're like a little old lady behind the wheel."

"Hazel, for shame," said Villon. "You're still mad at me. I thought in the time it took to drive here you'd be reassessing my assets and realize you have been badly misjudging me." He chucked her under the chin. "Think of Christmas and smile." Jim was at the front door, pressing the doorbell. "Ah!" said Villon, "chimes. How melodic and soothing." No one came to the door.

Mallory pushed the doorbell again. Hazel gently moved him to one side and tried the doorknob. The door opened.

"Hazel," said Villon, "this is breaking and entering."

"Even when I'm with two of the city's finest?" She pushed the door open and indicated for Mallory and Villon to lead the way. Mallory led them into the smartly albeit simply furnished downstairs hall.

Mallory shouted, "Hello? Anybody home?" There was no response. He looked at Villon and Hazel and shrugged. He indicated a room to the left. "That's where Claire holds court. Combination living room and library."

"Which way's the kitchen?" asked Hazel. "I'm famished."

"Don't you dare raid her refrigerator," admonished Villon. "I've often been warned that's a woman's most private territory." He took her hand and they followed Mallory into a room that Villon knew he could always be comfortable in. Yes, this was a room whose furnishings and decor had been overseen by Audrey Manners. It instantly brought back the memory of Audrey's charming cottage in Culver City, a short distance from M.G.M. Books, books, and more books. The Bible he saw was probably the very same one on which she had made him place his hand and promise to love her forever. The prints were in impeccable taste. It was a room a woman had furnished to please a man. And an awful lot of men must have been pleased in this room. He stared at Jim Mallory, who seemed transfixed. He was staring past a group of chairs to a fireplace in which no fire burned. Villon felt a sinking feeling in the pit of his stomach. He let Hazel's hand drop and advanced to Mallory's side.

Hazel didn't mind the dropping of her hand because she had noticed something the men had not yet seen. The desk had been ransacked, its contents spilled onto the floor. A row of bookshelves they wouldn't have seen when they entered the room were in disorder. Someone had been looking for something which she hoped he hadn't found. Prints and paintings hung awry on the walls. Somebody was looking for a wall safe.

Hazel turned to Villon and Mallory. They were kneeling. "Somebody's been ransacking the joint," she announced.

"They've done worse than that," said Villon. "They've cracked open Fern Arnold's skull."

ELEVEN

$\mathcal{H}$azel regretted crossing the room to where Fern lay dead. It was an ugly sight. Fern's eyes were open, staring, seemingly, at the murder weapon, a bloodstained poker. Villon went into action immediately after closing the corpse's eyes. He ordered Mallory to phone for the coroner, the morgue's hearse, and a team of detectives to assist. Mallory hurried out to use the phone in their car, as Hazel had already commandeered the phone in the room. She gave the scoop to the *Los Angeles Times* despite the fact it was not the Hearst publication in which Louella's column appeared. Hazel's delivery was terse and quick. Though not a *Times* employee, she frequently serviced them as a free-lance and the editor she dealt with trusted her, knowing she was reliable. He turned her over to a rewrite man, one Hazel knew quite well and frequently shot pool with, and gave him the facts like a veteran. She rattled off quickly the six rules of journalism a reporter abided by: Who, What, When, Where, Why, and How. After which she phoned Louella, followed by Jimmy Fidler and Sidney Skolsky.

Outside in the unmarked police car, Mallory was a model of his own brand of efficiency. The officer he was talking to was a movie buff and therefore given to exclaiming "Wow!" and "Yeah!" and "Boy!" as he had seen in numerous films, long ago realizing that movie fiction was far more interesting and exciting than police reality.

Driving home from Amelia's Claire Young was trying to bring order to the various characters dancing about in her brain. There was Amelia reassuring her the typewritten pages were safely hidden; there was her lawyer, Ronald Derwitt, assuring her her will was in perfect order and that Fern Arnold was an excellent choice for executor; there was Mitchell Carewe offering her sleeping pills while professing undying love; and there was her crippled son in a wheelchair enumerating the desirability of a future in the desert. She slowed down as she reached her house and recognized Fern's car but not the other two parked behind it. Instinct told her there was something wrong in her house. She pulled up in front of Fern's car and recognized Jim Mallory in the front seat of the police car talking heatedly into the precinct intercom. She hurried from her car to Jim, who had signed off and gone to meet her.

"What's going on? What's wrong?"

Jim never hedged when there was bad news to be delivered. "Fern's dead."

Claire could feel the blood draining from her cheeks. Jim thought she was going to faint and grabbed hold of her. Claire whispered, "How?"

"She's been murdered. In the library. There's been some ransacking there and she must have walked in on it."

With an anguished cry, Claire pulled away from him and ran into the house. Mallory followed. She hurried into the library as Hazel was wrapping up a conversation with an Associated Press editor. Hazel said, "Don't look! Don't look!" but Claire was not to be forestalled. Villon's back was to Claire, but when he heard her cry out, he turned. She was transfixed by the body. Hazel was at her side with an arm around her waist making what were probably soothing noises but sounded like an attempt to give life to a stalled engine.

Villon stared at Claire. Mallory stared at Villon staring at Claire.

Surprisingly enough, Hazel continued to be preoccupied with attempting to calm Claire. She was also thinking of William Powell awaiting her presence in his suite at the Metro studios. She moved her head to find Villon and found him immediately and felt an invisible stab in her heart from the way he was looking at Claire. He was looking at Claire but he was seeing Audrey Manners. Mallory was wondering if he would ever look at a woman with the tenderness with which Villon was looking at Claire. And then Claire turned away from the body and her eyes locked with Villon's. She recognized him immediately. Heavier, older, but still handsome in his own rough way. Herb Villon was not easily forgotten. Villon could see she was having a problem and took charge of the situation, while hoping Hazel would exercise some discretion.

Villon said, "I'm terribly sorry, Miss Young. It looks to me as though she died instantly. She apparently caught the killer in the act of ransacking the room and in a panic he picked up a poker from the fireplace and struck her." Claire said nothing, she just stared at him, and Mallory in his mind was hearing Jeannette MacDonald and Nelson Eddy bearing down on "The Indian Love Call." Hazel had backed away from Claire and was lighting a cigarette. "From the state of those bookshelves behind you and your desk he knew what he was looking for." Claire's eyes never left Villon. She knew that what the murderer was looking for he would never find. "I suspect he parked his car further down the road and came to the house on foot." He said to Mallory, "He was methodical enough to wipe the hilt of the poker." He said to Hazel, "I suppose photographers and reporters will be descending on us in hordes."

Hazel said sweetly, "It goes with the territory." She said to Claire, "How's for some brandy?" Claire said nothing and Villon told Hazel the brandy was an excellent idea. He wanted one for himself but didn't ask for it. He needed a clear head, he needed to be unimpaired in his thinking. Hazel went to the bar while Villon said to Claire, "Why don't you sit down over there?" He indicated the chair she had sat in the previous evening, conversing with Fern.

Claire's eyes were misting. She opened her handbag, found a

handkerchief, and put it to use as she walked to the chair and sat. Hazel brought the brandy and placed it on the end table next to where Claire was sitting. They heard sirens in the distance and Villon was relieved at the sound. Claire sipped the brandy. Hazel was at the phone dialing Metro and William Powell. Mallory knew he should be doing something productive but couldn't think of what. Villon said to him, "Come on, Jim. Get a move on. Look around the room. Maybe the bastard dropped a clue."

Fat chance, thought Mallory but nodded to Villon and slowly paced the room. He then wondered if Fern Arnold might be lying on something but had no intention of moving her body to find out. She was not a pretty sight though fortunately there was not much blood splattered. It had been a swift blow. A very neat job.

Villon asked Claire, "Is there someone you'd like us to call for you?"

Claire said huskily, "She's lying on the floor."

And now they heard the violin. Freda Groba preceded Lazlo Biro and Lucy Rockefeller into the room. They had hurried home from the precinct to change their clothes and hightail it to Claire's to propose a deal with her to take over the business. On seeing Villon and Mallory, Freda said, "What are you doing here? Who are you pinching?"

"Fern's dead!" cried Claire as she left the chair and went to Freda. "She's been murdered!"

Freda emitted a howl that chilled Mallory's spine. She and Fern had taken an instant liking to each other. Lucy Rockefeller saw the body and put her hands over her mouth. She hurried to a bathroom she knew was just off the kitchen.

Lazlo stopped playing the violin and crossed himself. Freda and Claire embraced each other while Hazel said into the phone, "Bill, it's Hazel. Something awful's happened." She told him about Fern's murder.

"Why, that poor dear thing," said Powell as Myrna entered from his kitchenette with a jug of dry martinis.

"What poor dear thing?" asked Myrna. Powell told her about Fern's murder.

Myrna was aghast or about as aghast as Myrna ever got. "You mean the woman we saw last night at Griselda's Cage?" Powell nodded yes. "How awful! She was so young, so attractive." She poured two martinis. She took one to Powell and then returned to retrieve her own.

Powell was asking Hazel, "Is Claire all right?"

Hazel said, "That depends on how you define 'all right.' Right now she's weeping into the bosom of a young woman who I assume is one of her young ladies. She travels — so help me God — with a violinist."

"Ah!" said Powell. "That would be Freda Groba. She's Hungarian. Lazlo is her entourage. Put Claire on the phone. I want to talk to her."

"I don't think she's in any condition to talk."

"Tell her it's me. We're very fond of each other."

"If I must say so myself, I make a damned good martini," Myrna said.

While waiting for Claire, Powell sipped his drink. "You most certainly do, Mrs. Hornblow. One of your more agreeable assets."

Myrna asked, "Did you know the deceased well?"

"We've chatted. She was a very amiable young woman. Devoted to Claire."

"Then Claire didn't do it," said Myrna firmly.

"Hazel mentioned the room had been partially ransacked," said Powell.

"Aha!" said Myrna. "The little black book!"

"What about it?"

"You say 'ransacked' and the first thing that comes to my mind is the book. Why else ransack the place?"

"I said partially ransacked. I'm hearing sirens."

"Where?"

"On the phone. The cops have arrived. Ah! I hear a familiar voice giving orders. I do believe it's our friend Villon."

"François?"

"Herb." He said to Myrna, "I wonder if Hazel's forgotten me.

112

Oh dear. Lazlo is playing "The Music Goes 'Round and 'Round.' "

Myrna said, "That's hardly appropriate for a murder. I wonder if he knows 'Rock of Ages.' "

"Possibly, if it ever reached Hungary. Ah! Claire! Baby, this is dreadful."

Claire gripped the phone tightly. "I can't think, Bill. I'm paralyzed. The cops are here and the press have arrived outside but Herb won't let them in."

"Ah! Then it is Herb Villon's voice I recognize. He's a good cop, Claire. You can trust him." For the moment, Claire reserved comment. "Listen, I'm coming over."

"That doesn't sound like a good idea. The place is swarming with reporters, photographers, you know, the press and the newsreels. It could look bad for you. Metro wouldn't like it."

"Damn Metro!"

"I second the motion," cried Myrna heartily as she raised her glass.

Powell was struck with an idea. "Myrna Loy's here with me. I'll bring her. We'll say we're researching our next *Thin Man* movie."

"Excellent thinking, Mr. Powell," said Myrna, now at his dressing table and freshening her makeup.

Claire made no further effort to dissuade Powell and hung up.

Powell said to Myrna as he stood behind her, straightening his tie and then smoothing his hair, "Well, Miss Loy, we've got it at last."

"Got what?"

"What you've been insisting we sorely needed. We've got a corpse!"

Myrna stared at him in the mirror. "Now really, Bill, a dead woman is hardly cause for a celebration."

"I am not celebrating, nor am I crying hosannas. There was bound to be a murder sooner or later, and now that we've got one, let's make the most of it."

Myrna said softly, "He'll kill again."

Powell stared at her and said, "Oh."

"I don't think he meant to kill Fern Arnold. She was murdered in Claire's house."

"He was hunting for the book in Claire's house."

"And also possibly hunting for Claire. Killing two birds with one stone." Myrna arose. "I hope Detective Villon is as competent as you say he is. He's got a lot on his plate right now and I don't think it's all that digestible."

Powell guided her out of his suite. "We're going to be running the gamut of reporters and photographers. Be prepared."

"We've run that gamut before. We're veterans of the wars. Push on!"

Hazel Dickson had done her job well. She'd disseminated the news of Fern's murder in time for the evening editions, and it was already a flash item on the radio. It wasn't that Fern Arnold was a celebrity or a newsworthy personage, but it was her connection to Claire Young and the little black book that vastly enhanced her newsworthiness. Equally important, this wasn't any old murder, it was a Hollywood murder, prime meat for the vultures to pick over. Newspapers dug into their picture archives to see what they had on Fern Arnold from her brief youthful skirmish as a promising starlet at Metro. Editors assigned their sob sisters to pursue the angle of another young innocent gone bad in Hollywood, like grapes left unpicked on the vine.

The radio on a shelf behind the bar at Griselda's wasn't tuned too loudly, but it was loud enough for the customers at the bar to hear the startling news and begin speculating. Griselda stared at the radio while the bartender asked, "Wasn't she the dame in here last night with that doctor?"

Griselda nodded her head. She didn't speak because an unidentifiable sadness had overtaken her. The dead woman was someone she knew. She was a habitué at Griselda's Cage. Not every night or afternoon of the week but often enough to bring a cheery greeting from Griselda whenever she came in. She never came alone, always with someone. Sometimes one of Claire's girls, sometimes one of Claire's unmarried clients, and a few times with Claire herself.

She heard the bartender saying, "I'll bet last night she didn't dream today she'd be a corpse."

"That's not funny," snapped Griselda.

"I wasn't meaning it to be funny, Griselda. I'm just saying we don't know from one day to the next what's going to happen to us."

"Howie, I had no idea that under this roof I was harboring a philosopher."

Howie grinned. "Me? A philosopher? Well, I'll be damned."

"Probably," said Griselda as she went to greet a couple looking for a late lunch.

Outside Claire's house, the photographers and reporters were in a feeding frenzy, but there was little for them to feed on. Villon had assigned one of his veteran detectives, Zachary Forrest, to try and keep order among the gentlemen of the press. Forrest immediately assigned a detective to the other three sides of the house to keep the press from trying to trespass unnoticed. Some of the more enterprising reporters and photographers busied themselves photographing the house and grounds from all angles and ringing the doorbells of neighbors to see if they had noticed any suspicious-looking characters in the vicinity.

"Madam," a reporter asked a middle-aged woman whose bridge game he had interrupted, "have you seen anyone around here today that might have looked like a killer?"

"Just you," she snapped and slammed the door shut.

Inside Claire's house, the coroner's examination of Fern was a cursory one. He didn't need a diagram to illustrate to him that the blow to Fern's skull was all it took to kill her. He did comment that it was a vicious wound and it made Villon say to Mallory, "I wonder if she knew her killer."

"I wouldn't be the least surprised," said Mallory. "Leaving those french windows open is an invitation to anyone to come on in."

The french windows were at the opposite side of the room and Villon said, "It's a warm day. Fern must have opened them and maybe gone into the kitchen to fix something for herself. Everybody in this town leaves windows and doors open. Nobody thinks they might be inviting a criminal by making entry so easy."

Mallory said, "How many times have I seen a body being removed and why do I still get a queasy stomach?"

Freda crossed herself as the attendants carrying the stretcher onto which Fern's wrapped body was strapped passed her and Lazlo and Lucy Rockefeller, who turned her face away or risked a rapid return to the bathroom. Claire's eyes followed the stretcher out of the room. She was seated at her desk with her hands folded, fighting tears. She saw Villon go out of the room and got up to follow him. Hazel watched her and then lit a cigarette. Mother had warned her there might be days like this. She wished she wasn't jealous of a romance that had occurred about a decade ago. Mallory was talking to Freda Groba.

"What are you doing here?" he asked her.

"I came to talk business with Claire. I did not expect to find murder."

"What kind of business?"

"Prostitute business, vot other kind is there to discuss? But I suppose now is not the time. But we'll stay with Claire for a while. Now is not the time for her to be alone. You agree?"

"Freda," said Mallory, feeling in his gut there was worse to come, "I most certainly agree."

T W E L V E

Claire followed Villon to an enclosed porch off the front hall which afforded privacy from prying eyes by a row of tall, thickly grown hedges. Claire sat in a wicker chair while Villon leaned against the wall with his arms folded. Claire asked, "Who was it that phoned the police?"

"Nobody phoned us. A couple of hours ago Jim Mallory and I were batting suppositions back and forth. About you, the black book, your abrupt defection from the business. We agreed you had set yourself up to be murdered."

Claire found a cigarette in her handbag, lit it, popped the lighter back in the handbag, and snapped it shut. She exhaled smoke and then their eyes met. Hers were not unkindly. "That's a pretty crazy idea."

"Not if you carry insurance with a double indemnity clause." She stared at the lighted end of the cigarette. "And in case you don't know, a double indemnity clause means there's no pay-off if the subject committed suicide." He paused and then took the plunge. "You want to be killed so there'll be a pay-off. I'm not asking who to, it's none of my business. Are you that seriously ill?"

"I never heard of anyone being ill just for the fun of it. I have an inoperable cancer and my timetable is cutting it too close for me to kid around."

"Which is why you put out the news about the book. You figured someone would come gunning for you."

"That's right. Only it was Fern who took the heat . . ." She fought back tears. "What a dirty trick I played on myself. Fern! My best friend. The only person I could really trust. And how would you like a laugh? She's the executor of my will!" She took a long drag on the cigarette while Villon studied her face. Still beautiful, the skin as lovely as ever, no telltale lines, not a sign of illness, even more beautiful than when he first met and fell in love with her. He heard Claire ask, "What are you looking for?"

"I found it. The pretty kid I met a long time ago."

Claire deftly sidestepped the remark. "You came out here because you and Jim decided I had set myself up to be killed. And how did you think you could prevent it?"

"That remains to be discussed."

"There's nothing to discuss."

"You're in danger and with Fern murdered in your house that makes it a case for the police. You may want to get yourself bumped off but it's my job to see that you don't."

"If you're thinking of setting up watchdogs to protect me, you can forget it." She stubbed out the cigarette in an ashtray. "Hazel's in love with you, right?"

"On a clear day."

"She knows I was Audrey Manners."

"Hazel's a very smart lady."

"Well, tell her to stop following my every move as though I might think of running off with you. You're the past, Herb, and I don't live in the past. Not that I wouldn't trade the present for a hope of a future but I never kidded myself about anything and I'm not about to start now." She got up.

"Why is Audrey Manners supposed to be such a mystery?"

"Because she's the past. She had nineteen pretty good years and could have had more if she hadn't screwed up. Claire Young's done pretty damn well for herself and Claire Young could use a stiff drink." She turned on her heel and walked away from him briskly.

A few minutes later Jim Mallory found him. "The forensics squad is here. They're dusting the place. What about the book? You find out where she's hidden it?"

"You know, Jim. I didn't even think of asking her."

"Bill, sometimes you're so damned clever," said Myrna to Powell as he tooled along in his custom-built Cadillac convertible, "I never *heard* of double indemnity. How'd you know about it?"

"My insurance agent told me about it after I got some new policies when I divorced Carole. He thought I was all broken up about it and toying with suicide."

"How could anybody think of you committing suicide? The very idea!"

"Well now, Mrs. Hornblow, that's very sweet of you. But there have been times when I've entertained the notion of doing away with myself."

"I don't believe you. Not you. Never."

"Never say never. I believe there's a song on the subject."

Myrna wore a shawl wrapped around her head to protect her hair from the wind, Powell having commented she looked like a very chic Ukrainian peasant. "Claire Young is a very courageous woman."

"Why?"

"Setting herself up to be murdered! That takes courage!"

"There are those who might call it an act of idiotic stupidity."

"Well, I'm not among them," said Myrna. "Of course, I have no sympathy for suicide."

"Why? Did someone near and dear have a go at it?"

"Goodness no. My father died in the great flu epidemic of 1919. Bill, are you sure you're going in the right direction?"

"I'm quite sure. And if I've forgotten the way, which is hardly likely, my trusty Cadillac convertible can find its way there on its own. This clever mechanical marvel has gotten me safely home when I've been in no condition to drive. Why one morning after a wild night at Charlie Chaplin's — one of his typical nights of nubile nymphets and much champagne *sec* and *brut* and the host's monumental ego — I awakened in my bachelor's boudoir stretched out in bed in a very wrinkled tuxedo. It took me some time to realize I was in my own bed in my very own bedroom. But the Cadillac, I worried, in what condition is the Cadillac? I made my way downstairs with, of course, some difficulty because the house seemed to be swaying — "

"Earthquake?" asked a concerned Myrna, who was convinced they were traveling in the wrong direction.

"No silly, monumental hangover. Anyway, there in the garage was this dependable old darling, and you know what?"

"No, what?"

"I had washed it!" She flashed him a look of skepticism. "So help me Hannah. Ah! Look ahead! Police cars! Newsreel trucks! Reporters! Camera men! Detectives protecting the house like Cerberus at the gate. Off with the shawl, Minnie. Murder will out, as they say, but movie stars have got to be eternally glamorous. Off with the shawl."

"I'll have you know it's a Schiaparelli made especially for me by Elsa herself as a personalized gift. She doesn't market shawls as a rule, you know. Oy oy oy, here comes the conquering horde! Smile! Let's look affable."

"Don't be silly. This is a very sad occasion. Now remember. We're here to do research." Powell parked and Myrna removed the shawl. As they got out of the car, they were immediately recognized and surrounded, mercilessly bombarded with questions while the cameras rolled.

Powell shouted, "Ladies and gentlemen of the press! Come to order, please. We are here quite unofficially. We are doing research for our next *Thin Man* movie."

"What's the title?" shouted a reporter.

"Title? Title? Minnie, do you remember the title?"

"Me? Remember the title? Oh sure. *The Thin Man's Dandruff.*" They were having difficulty reaching the front door.

"Hey Bill!" yelled a reporter. "Does Louis B. Mayer know you know Claire Young?"

"I keep nothing from Mr. Mayer. He's like an uncle to me. Uncle Louis."

"Hey Myrna. Are you and Hornblow split for good?"

"No," riposted Myrna, "we're split for bad."

A sob sister asked, "You giving him a Christmas present?"

"Oh heavens no," said Myrna, enjoying herself immensely. "The whole point of the separation was to avoid giving him a Christmas gift."

Inside the house, Villon had told Mallory to see what all the fuss was outside. Mallory checked and reported that Loy and Powell had arrived.

"Who invited them?" asked Villon.

Claire spoke up. "Bill Powell is a very good friend of mine. He volunteered to come here with Miss Loy."

Villon asked in exasperation, "Is this a murder case or a three-ring circus?"

Hazel Dickson had hurried to the front door to greet the stars. On opening the door she found them detained by the detective assigned to stand guard there. Powell was insisting, "Let us by, we're expected."

Hazel tapped the detective on the shoulder. "They're expected," she corroborated, "to give aid and comfort." The detective reluctantly stood to one side, thoroughly unimpressed by the celebrity of the stars. Hazel gushed at the stars as she led them inside the house and Myrna wondered what the woman was thinking of dyeing her hair that awful red color. Myrna's hair was a true, shimmering red, and she would permit Sidney Guileroff, the Metro hair stylist, only to touch it up with the highlights necessary for the cameras.

Claire hurried to Powell, who embraced her, hugging her tightly. "Go ahead and cry, dear, it's good for the ducts."

"I'm all cried out," said Claire. "Thanks for coming." She said to Myrna, "I remember meeting you under happier circumstances."

"There'll be other happier circumstances," said Myrna and then her eyes widened in amazement at hearing a violin rendition of "There'll Be a Hot Time in the Old Town Tonight." Claire explained Lazlo and introduced Myrna to Freda and Lucy who were genuinely delighted to meet her. "Oh, there's François Villon," said Myrna.

"Herb Villon," corrected Powell.

"Oh yes, of course!" They shook hands with Villon, of whom Myrna then said with perspicacity, "He's not really glad to see us. You're not, Mr. Villon, are you?"

"This is a murder investigation," said Villon, "not dinner at the Mocambo."

"We understand that, Mr. Villon. We are here on Claire's behalf." She looked around. "Now then, what have you done with the corpse?"

Villon said, "What we usually do with a corpse. Send it to the morgue to be autopsied with an identification tag around the big toe."

Myrna said with her patented charm, "I'm sure you don't mean to be ungracious, Mr. Villon."

"You're right. I'm sorry. I don't mean to be," and he managed a smile.

"I think Bill and I are going to surprise you and be of some help." Villon groaned inwardly. "We've been doing a lot of theorizing on our way here. For example, I assume you've heard of the double indemnity clause in insurance policies?" She didn't miss the look Villon flashed to Claire. "I see you have." She turned to Claire. "Claire, I was telling Bill on the drive here how much I admire you. It takes the kind of guts I don't think I'll ever have to set yourself up as a target for a murderer. Oh dear, you look chagrined." She said to Villon, "But that's what it's all about, isn't it?"

Bill Powell said to her, "Minnie dear, slow down a bit."

"Why?" she asked, batting her eyelashes. "I'm just getting warmed up. And I can tell our theories are good because Hazel is taking notes. I'm not going too fast for you, am I, Hazel?"

Powell said, "Nobody ever goes too fast for Hazel." Villon tacitly agreed while Hazel kept writing in her pad, her handbag held tightly under her left arm.

Myrna asked Villon, "How do you suppose the killer got in the house? Do you suppose Fern knew him and opened the front door to him, which is rather ridiculous as he'd undoubtedly come to find the little black book and that being the case, he certainly doesn't want anyone to know his identity. He obviously didn't succeed because Claire seems to be upset only by Miss Arnold's murder. I mean, Mr. Villon, when she came home and saw that a section of the room and her desk had been ransacked, she didn't check to see the book was still safely hidden, that is, if it's hidden in this room." She smiled. "I'll bet it is."

Powell suavely moved closer to Myrna and said under his breath, "Minnie, try putting a lid on it for a while. I think Villon is finding you a bit tiresome."

Myrna feigned astonishment. She was very self-assured about their theories. "Mr. Villon, I'll bet we're on the same wavelength. If we aren't, I'll go away and powder my nose."

"A very lovely nose," said Villon, and Hazel looked up from her pad, "and some pretty damned good theorizing."

Myrna turned to Bill with a look of triumph, "Now how's that for generosity!" She smiled at Villon. "You're a good sport, Mr. Villon. And I'm having a perfectly marvelous time. Shall I go on or shall I shut up?"

"Hell no," said Villon.

"Hell no, go on or hell no, shut up?"

"Please continue, Miss Loy. You might come up with something I haven't thought of. Detectives aren't infallible."

Hazel said, "Myrna Loy, don't you dare stop. This is going to make a terrific feature story."

Myrna suggested, "Be sure to mention the Nick and Nora Charles angle. That'll keep Metro happy because they're going to be pretty miserable when they find out we're here."

Powell asked, "And how will they find out we're here?"

"Oh Bill, you can be so unbecomingly dense at times. With that gang of reporters and photographers out there, every one of whom would betray their country for an in with our Howard Strickling — he's Mayer's henchman," she explained to the room in general, while smiling at Lazlo, who had launched into a schmaltzy rendition of "As Time Goes By" — "Louis B. knows or will soon know. Mr. Villon, do all murder investigations have musical accompaniment?"

"Is it annoying you?" asked Villon.

"Oh heavens, no. I find it enchanting. Bill, have you anything to contribute, dear?"

"You keep right at it, Minnie. You're doing splendidly. Don't you agree, Claire?" Claire was mesmerized by a detective covering the bloodied carpet near the fireplace with an oilcloth. "Claire?"

Her head jerked up. "What?"

"Don't you think Myrna is doing splendidly?"

"Splendidly." Powell crossed to her and put an arm around her shoulders. Claire was anxious to phone her aunt out in Venice Beach. They must have heard the news of Fern's death by now, though her son wasn't big for newscasts. Maidie would be upset, worried, even frantic. No, never frantic. Maidie was too level-headed for that. If Maidie had heard, she would have phoned by now.

Myrna was standing at the french windows. "The killer must have gotten in through these french windows."

"They were open when we got here," said Jim Mallory.

"I was wondering if you'd ever say anything," said Myrna. "You have to be a detective. No reporters permitted on the premises." Jim reminded her they had met when she came to the precinct for some instruction on police procedure for *Whipsaw*. Myrna didn't remember him but sweetly said she did. Mallory wondered if it made sense to fall in love with her despite the fact she was married, albeit, from what he discerned, at the present somewhat shakily.

Powell asked hopefully, "Myrna, have you finished?"

"Good heavens, no," she said in a tone of voice meant to scold him. Her hands were on her hips while for a brief moment she wished Powell would make up his mind. First he says she's doing splendidly and several breaths later he's wondering if she's finished.

"So here we are at the french windows through which it's more than likely that he got into the house unheard by Fern, who was probably busy elsewhere. This charming young man," — she indicated Mallory — "said they were open when you people arrived."

"Which 'you people'?" asked Powell.

"Oh now really, Bill. Mr. Mallory and of course Mr. Villon and most assuredly Hazel. The musical accompaniment and friends had to have arrived later. So he made his entrance through the french windows."

"Or his exit," suggested Villon in a very firm voice.

"Well," said Myrna, with her trademark wrinkle of the nose, "let's assume he did both. Don't you agree, Mr. Villon?"

THIRTEEN

*T*o the intoxicating strains of a wild *czardas,* one of the forensics experts wrapped the poker while Hazel assured Claire there was an excellent product on the market that removed bloodstains from rugs. Claire was appalled, and finally rescued by the ringing of the telephone. It was Maidie and she was relieved to hear Claire's voice.

"Are you all right? We just got back from shopping. We just heard it on the news." She lowered her voice. "Elmer knows nothing. He's listening to a serial. *John's Other John* or something like that. I can't tell one from the other. Now listen to me, Claire, you're not safe in that house. You get out. Go to a hotel where there are lots of people. Please, Claire, please listen to me, I'm frightened."

Claire reassured her. "I'm not alone." She didn't say she wished she was. Myrna caught the irony in Claire's voice. "I'm surrounded by admirers. Reporters, photographers, newsreel people, an assortment of detectives, and William Powell and Myrna Loy."

Maidie didn't believe that at all. "Oh, go on with you! How can you crack jokes at a time like this?"

Claire resumed reassuring Maidie. "I won't be alone tonight. Three friends are going to stay with me. Yes, one plays the violin. One's a mad Hungarian with a heart of gold she'll probably one day hock, and another is her best friend, who's having stomach trouble. I'll call you tonight. God bless." She hung up. She said to Myrna, "My aunt Maidie. She lives in Venice."

"Oh, I'm so glad you have a relative. I was so afraid you were alone in the world, like anybody out here whose option was suddenly dropped. Bill Powell, why are you snooping around that desk?" He was on his hands and knees tapping the wood that masked the back of the desk.

"This piece of furniture might just have a hidden drawer. There was a desk like that in *The Emperor's Candlesticks.*"

"Fiddlesticks," said Myrna.

"Minnie, there's no cause for you to be contrary. I was in that picture. You weren't." He resumed tapping.

Myrna said to Villon, "I'm sure you should probably be doing what Bill's doing."

Villon said knowledgeably, "I don't think we'll see that black book until Claire decides to show it to us. If she's ever going to show it to us. If it even exists."

"Oh, it exists all right," said Myrna with remarkable self-assurance. "You can attribute that to women's intuition. I keep a diary. Nothing much to interest the prurient, meaning anyone with a dirty mind, like my husband." She thought for a moment. "Well, it isn't exactly a dirty mind. But Arthur is very jealous, very suspicious, and highly competitive. He's also a chronic flirt and I'd love to see that book of Claire's because I suspect Arthur is in it."

"She's here in the room. Why don't you ask her?"

"That'd be putting her on the spot. She's having a bad enough time as it is. If it was me I'd be flat on my back on the chaise longue in my bedroom with smelling salts in one hand and a gin martini in the other and wondering why had God forsaken me."

"Aud . . . Claire's made of sterner stuff," said Villon.

"You speak with such assurance. Why do I suspect you go a long way back with Claire?"

"I don't know, why do you?"

"Earlier she wasn't too subtle about indicating she wanted you to follow her out of the room. And it wasn't for protection."

"Miss Loy . . ."

"Mr. Villon, please call me Myrna and I'll call you François . . ."

"The name's Herb."

"Oh, I'm so sorry, of course it is. And I'll call you Herb. And you can call Mr. Powell Bill and . . . Look, he's found something. A slip of paper. What have you got there, Bill?"

"A slip of paper. I found it under the desk."

Claire crossed to him. He read what was written on the paper and gave it to Claire. "Here you are, my dear. I believe it's a prescription written by Doctor Carewe. I can't make head or tail of it. It's in doctor hieroglyphics."

"It was in one of the drawers," said Claire. "One of the ransacked drawers."

"Which explains what it was doing under your desk." He said to Villon and Myrna, "It's dated yesterday."

"It should be. That's when I saw him. It's a prescription for sleeping pills. I haven't been sleeping well lately. Don't let sleeping pills worry you, Herb. I know all about double indemnity clauses. Besides, it was Mitchell who suggested I have them."

Myrna asked Bill, "Wasn't that the name of the doctor we saw with Fern Arnold last night at Griselda's?"

"Yes." Bill said archly to Claire, "Griselda fingered him. Were Fern and the doctor what they call an item?"

Claire said icily, "Fern and no one were an item. Not lately." She walked away from them to Freda and Lucy, and Lazlo serenaded the room with "Did You Ever See a Dream Walking?"

Lucy said to Lazlo, "Oh, not that one again." He swiftly segued to "With My Eyes Wide Open I'm Dreaming."

Claire said to the women, "Would you be sweethearts and set up a pot of coffee? There's all sorts of sandwich stuff in the fridge. I can't believe I'm hungry but I'm hungry."

Jim Mallory overheard Claire and went to Hazel. "There's going to be sandwiches and coffee."

"Oh, thank God. My stomach's been rumbling."

Detective Zachary Forrest came into the house and went to Villon. Villon asked, "What's up?"

"Some members of the press are complaining why does Hazel Dickson have special privileges."

Villon was annoyed. He didn't like reporters and he didn't like photographers, having been misquoted often enough in the past to make him leery of the lot. Hazel was no exception despite his love for her and he had told her so often that he'd stopped repeating himself ages ago because he knew all his reprimands fell on deaf ears. He told Forrest, "Hazel was with us when we found the body. Tell them she's claiming squatter's rights." Forrest nodded and left.

Powell was saying to Myrna, "Minnie, you're mumbling something."

"No I'm not. I've acquired your favorite habit, talking to oneself."

"And what are you telling yourself?"

"I'm telling myself not to be such a damn fool."

"And why, if I may be so bold to ask, are you telling yourself not to be such a damn fool?"

"I think I'm suffering from the *Thin Man* syndrome."

"I didn't think there was such a thing."

"It's similar to that old murder mystery chestnut."

"Are you thinking of *Cherchez la femme*?"

"As a matter of fact, that will do nicely too. What I've actually been thinking about is that other murder mystery chestnut, the least likely suspect."

"Myrna, what we have here is the prospect of several hundred suspects."

"Don't be ridiculous."

"I'm not being in the least bit ridiculous. Every man who has used Claire's services I should think would contemplate homicide to keep that little black book from exposing their indiscretions."

"Balderdash."

"Oh, I like that word! What made you think of it?"

"It just popped into my head. You know how things are always popping into my head. Let's go to the french windows. I don't want to be overheard."

"There's a detective stationed out there near them. Aren't you worried he might overhear?"

"You don't speak French, do you?"

"No I don't. And neither do you."

"I most certainly do. Some. Arthur and I picked it up when we spent that time in Paris when I was under suspension last year."

"And what else did Arthur pick up?"

She ignored that as she walked casually to the windows, Powell keeping step with her. At the windows, he looked out. "Why, it's a fenced-in garden. How pretty. Don't you agree, Minnie? We're in luck. The detective's on the other side of the fence. And so here we are and from the look on Villon's face I think he's curious to know what we're up to."

"I'm sure he is. He thinks I'm awfully good at theory. Wave him over to join us. But subtly. The others might get suspicious."

"Well, we certainly can't have that, can we?"

"We certainly can't."

Villon went to join Powell and Myrna, unnoticed by Hazel, who was deep in conversation with Jim Mallory while Claire seemingly was standing guard over the forensics people dusting her bookshelves.

Powell said to Villon when he joined them, "Strange little case you've got here, Herb."

"Very strange and not all that little. Well?"

"Well what?"

"What are you two up to?"

Myrna said, "I'm the one who's up to something. Bill's not up to a thing, at least not that I know of."

Powell said, "Myrna is entertaining a theory about the least likely suspect."

Villon stated flatly, "The fiddler."

"Oh, never him," said Myrna.

"You're right. Because at the time of the murder he was behind bars with Freda and Lucy. They even let him share their cell though it's a strict rule in our local lock-ups that men and women must be segregated."

"Louis B. Mayer would approve strongly of that. He's a stickler for segregation. Black actors are only hired at Metro to play menials. When I brought it to his attention — much, I might add, to his discomfort — he called me a 'Bolshevik.' Anyway, I don't consider Lazlo or the ladies suspects, though it's tempting because the three of them certainly come under the heading of least likely. Now listen carefully and don't pass judgment until I'm finished." She looked around to make sure no one else was within earshot. Then she said softly, "Claire Young."

For the first time in a long time, Villon appeared dumbfounded. Myrna asked, "Cat got your tongue?"

Powell said, "I must say, Minnie darling, you've managed to roll *Cherchez la femme* and the least likely suspect into one rather untidy little package. I don't see Claire murdering her best friend and confidante. I don't see Claire murdering anyone."

Myrna stood her ground though she was beginning to see it was a bit shaky. "What's the matter with you two? Have you never suffered betrayal by a supposed best friend? I'm sorry I've upset you, Herb, I can see you harbor a Grade A quality of loyalty. And it's quite obvious you've still got a soft spot in your heart for Audrey Manners. A little while ago you started to say Audrey was made of sterner stuff, but you caught yourself and substituted Claire for Audrey. She was obviously very important in your past and I think she still is. I know now there's Hazel and has been for a long time and she's quite a girl. But Herb, you can't close your mind to a suspicion just because it involves someone you care about."

"You're right, Myrna. If it'll make you feel better, Claire's on my list too." Myrna felt better. "I suppose you have a scenario as to how Claire might have done it?"

"Well, yes I do. It goes something like this. Claire comes home sometime around noon. Fern didn't expect her back so soon and is hunting for the black book in the library. Claire surprises Fern. Fern didn't hear her coming in." She took a dramatic pause. "Fern has found the book and Claire is outraged." She paused, her eyes darting back and forth between the two men.

"Go on," said Villon.

"By all means, Minnie," said Powell.

"You're laughing at me," said Myrna.

"Not at all. I'm fascinated. I'm completely in your thrall."

"I don't care what you're in. We saw Fern and the doctor together last night. They looked as though they were cooking up something."

"That could be one interpretation," said Powell. "It also could have been a very innocent, matter-of-fact *tête-à-tête*."

"It's not much of a *tête-à-tête* when they order drinks and don't order dinner and she flounces out leaving him alone at the table." She said to Herb, "That's exactly what happened. I'm positive the friends who were with us can corroborate that."

"I believe you, Myrna," said Herb. "But I can't see Claire hitting Fern over the head with the poker. Myrna, for me it doesn't play."

"Me either, Minnie. It needs a rewrite."

"I'm sorry I started this thing. I'm beginning to feel like a fool."

"You're not a fool, Minnie." Powell said, "You're a very smart cookie who might have gone off on the wrong tangent. Everyone's entitled to that."

"But you haven't let me finish!" Myrna's cheeks were flushed with annoyance. "I know, I know. I sound a little carried away and overwrought having been caught up in this investigation. Herb, I'm only trying to be of help. Is my theory so completely illogical to you?"

"The hell of it is," said Herb, "it's a possibility. Claire's under heavy pressure what with her illness, the little black book, money worries. If Fern found the book Claire could see herself being betrayed. She might even go berserk and attack her with the poker. But I was here when Claire came home; her reaction to Fern lying battered in a pool of blood was genuine horror and heartbreak. And I suspect Claire was never that good an actress. What I saw was genuine." Then he gave a Gallic shrug. "But who knows?" He caught Claire's eye and gestured her to join them. He said to Myrna, "Let me handle this."

"Of course," said Myrna. "You're in charge."

Claire joined them. "What is it, Herb?"

"Claire, where were you all morning until you came home?"

Claire cottoned immediately. "You don't think I might have killed Fern?"

"Claire, you know it's my job to cover all trails."

"Sure, Herb, sure. I was at Amelia Hubbard's. She's a free-lance secretary. I was giving dictation. She usually comes here but her car was on the fritz. So I went to her. I was with her from around ten in the morning until I left to come back here. I'll give you Amelia's number. You can phone and ask her."

"Thanks, Claire. I believe you. Myrna?"

"Of course I do. I'm sorry, Claire. I must be suffering from a bad case of *The Thin Man*. I've gotten carried away and I hereby resign." She said to Powell, "So there."

"So there what?"

"So there I resign, that's what."

"Why?"

"Why what?"

"Why do you resign, Minnie? Since when are you a quitter? I'm ashamed of you, Minnie, ashamed that you'd turn in your badge when the department needs you the most. You want her to resign, Herb?"

"Hell no, the way she thinks she just might come up with the murderer after all."

Myrna said, "Claire, forgive me. But I have a habit of coming up with some very strange theories."

Claire found a smile. "Maybe one of them will turn out to be not all that strange."

Myrna was delighted. "Why Claire, that's terribly kind of you.

Now look, dear, let me help you. I've got some time on my hands. I'm talking about funeral arrangements for Fern. Notifying her family."

"How nice of you," said Claire, "but Freda and Lucy are looking after everything. They're quite competent."

"Oh, Freda's very competent," said Powell.

"I'm sure you speak from experience," said Myrna.

Claire excused herself and went to the kitchen to see how the ladies were doing with the sandwiches and coffee.

Myrna said to the men, "I suppose you think I made a complete fool of myself."

"Not at all," said Herb. "Quite honestly, I've been wondering what Fern was up to seeing Mitchell Carewe last night. You see, Claire and Mitchell were once quite an item. Years ago when she was at Metro and he was interning."

Powell asked, "Do Claire and Fern go that far back?"

"Of course they do," said Myrna.

"You're so sure?" asked Powell.

"I could swear I heard someone say they met at Metro." She thought for a moment. "I was at Metro then. My first time around at Metro. The hell with it. Herb, what about Mitchell Carewe? What do you know about him?"

"His medical reputation is impeccable."

"Oh," said Myrna dejectedly.

"Now what?" asked Powell.

"I was hoping he was a quack."

Villon told her, "He has a very imposing list of movie star clientele."

Myrna said, "That doesn't make him good. It only makes him successful."

"Nothing wrong with that," said Powell.

Jim Mallory joined them and asked Villon, "Any point in the forensics boys dusting the rest of the house?"

"A waste of time. This is the only room where it's necessary. Are you telling me they're finished in here?"

"Hell no. They just weren't looking forward to doing more than this room. Are you going to let me in on what was going on with Claire Young?"

Herb told him, "Myrna saw her as a possible suspect."

"Why not?" said Mallory jovially, "the more the merrier."

"She's got an alibi," said Myrna. "Amelia something."

"Amelia Hubbard," said Herb. He told Mallory, "She's a freelance secretary. Claire was giving dictation."

Myrna was deep in thought. "Now what do you suppose Claire was dictating?"

Powell said with a broad grin, "What does every madam in captivity dictate sooner or later? Her memoirs."

Myrna brightened, "Oh Bill, do you think?"

"I do not merely think, I hope. I hope she is. I can't wait to read them."

Villon shook his head and said somewhat glumly, "Memoirs on top of a little black book. Excuse me." He went in search of Claire. He found her in the kitchen where she was helping Freda and Lucy with the sandwiches. Lazlo had set his violin aside to concentrate on a dill pickle. Villon spoke to Claire and she followed him out of the kitchen into the front hall where they could have some privacy. "Have you been dictating your memoirs?"

"Smart deduction."

"Not mine. Bill Powell deserves the credit. Now listen, Claire, I hate to think that what you're working on is a soupçon of blackmail."

"Has anyone complained to the police that I'm blackmailing them?"

"Not that I've heard so far."

"And you won't hear." Her chin was lifted and defiant. "What I have received are contributions from various gentleman to help cover the costs of my illness. And I might add, they were unsolicited. And don't ask me for names because you won't get them."

"Well, little Audrey — "

"The name is Claire."

"Okay, the name is Claire. But let me let you in on a fresh theory of mine. You want so badly to be murdered, then you missed your golden opportunity today. You should have stayed home, because I have an idea Fern was the wrong victim. The killer mistook her for you."

"Baloney. If it's anyone who knows us, he'd know Fern, we're no more alike than Laurel and Hardy."

"And not nearly as funny."

"Nice try, Herb. And don't push the blackmail bit. I've got a very shrewd lawyer. And as for the existence of my little black book, it's right there in the library. Right under everybody's nose. And you'll never find it. Not you, not anyone. Anything else."

"Maybe once upon a time, but not today."

FOURTEEN

$\mathcal{L}$ouis B. Mayer lay flat on his back on the floor of his office with his eyes shut and his mouth open. In his left hand he tightly clutched the French-style telephone he'd been holding when he heard the news that sent him into a faint. Ida Koverman stood over him, hands on hips, looking down at her prostrate employer. Howard Strickling, Mayer's favorite henchman, was at the bar pouring a tumbler of Southern Comfort, Mayer's favorite drink. Ida said over her shoulder to Strickling, "Did you see that pirouette when he leapt out of the chair? Pure Nijinski. I wonder what it was that sent him flying and then into his swoon?"

Mayer's eyes fluttered open. Ida looked down at him while thinking, The fraud. He had no more fainted than she had. His mouth closed slowly and then his tongue flicked out, obscenely moistening his lips. And then he croaked, "Seltzer."

Ida turned to Strickling. "Hold the Southern Comfort. He wants seltzer."

Strickling downed the Southern Comfort and grabbed a seltzer bottle and a tall glass. Ida wondered if the sound of the syphon was music to Mayer's ears. She heard him say, "Where am I?"

"Where you always are when you faint. Do you want me to help you up or would my assistance make you question your manhood?"

"Ida, you've got a real rotten mouth." With an effort, he sat up. He grabbed hold of the desk top and pulled himself to his feet. Strickling was at his side with the glass of seltzer. Mayer sat behind his desk, placed the telephone where it belonged, then grasped the glass of seltzer and gulped it down greedily. He slammed the empty glass on the desk, burped lavishly while both Koverman and Strickling shut their eyes and then bellowed, "I have been betrayed!"

"Again?" asked Koverman. She lifted the empty glass and asked Mayer, "You want more?"

"I want the heads of William Powell and Myrna Loy on a salver!" His arms were raised, his fists were clenched, the veins stood out on his neck, and Ida began to worry the old fraud might be giving himself a genuine fit of apoplexy.

Strickling too was concerned. "What have they done, boss?"

"Done? Done? They have betrayed me. Oh, what an awful day I'm having. What a terrible day." He stared at the ceiling. "God!" he commanded, "How have I offended thee?"

The "thee" sent Ida's eyebrows up an inch. She said in one of her occasional motherly tones, "I'm sure you're overreacting. I can't think of anything you've done today that might offend Him, and from what I hear tell at my local convent, He doesn't offend easily." She said to Strickling, "After all, He doesn't dare let the milk of human kindness curdle too often."

Strickling couldn't care less about the ways of His Supreme Highness; Powell and Loy were two of his favorite people. They had class. They were urbane. They were witty in their own unique way and most important of all, they were big box office with a legion of fans across the world. "What have Bill and Myrna done that can't be undone?"

"You bet your *pupik* it can't be undone, because what they've done is on film!"

Oh my God, thought Ida, they've finally had sex together and

138

somebody's caught it on film. There were two things Ida thoroughly disapproved of, Louis B. Mayer and sex. Mayer, because although he had placed her in a position of power as his assistant with a very handsome salary, she loathed his exploitation of young women and the way he could blithely bring a career crashing down around an actor's ears. It was no secret that he loathed, among others, Wallace Beery and Jean Harlow, but they were at the top of the heap and not easily dispossessed. He'd had his opportunity to wreck Harlow's career when her second husband, Paul Bern, was found dead in their home under suspicious circumstances. But it was at a time when Harlow had turned the tide of her career into the big time. So that was one of several reasons why he disapproved of Harlow. As for sex, Ida hadn't been offered any since the age of thirteen when she played You Show Me Yours and I'll Show You Mine with her perverted cousin Mervyn, who later made a fortune during Prohibition as a bootlegger.

She heard Strickling asking, "What can't be undone? What's on film?"

Mayer made fists and slammed his desk with them. "They're with the hoor!"

"Which hoor?" asked Strickling, but in his heart knowing the answer he was about to hear.

"Which hoor? Which hoor he asks me? Claire Young the hoor! Whoever that killer is, he murdered the wrong one!"

Ida said, "What he's telling us is that two of his stars are apparently giving aid and comfort to the enemy."

"They've been photographed by every goddamn newsreel in this rotten town! The newspapers have nailed them! The media is growing fat from the Thin Man and his co-star." He leapt out of his chair and started pacing the room. "I'll punish them! Oh God, how I'll punish them! I'll lend them to Republic Pictures." Then he thought and stormed, "Worse! I'll lend them to Monogram!" Republic and Monogram were two of the most successful third-rate producers of cheap quickies.

Ida reminded him, "The last time you punished a star, you

loaned Clark Gable to Columbia Pictures for *It Happened One Night* and he won an Academy Award and now Columbia is almost as powerful as we are.''

Mayer couldn't stand being reminded. He spat a word at Ida: ''Fishwife!'' Then he turned on Strickling. ''Howard! Don't just stand there! Do something!''

Strickling was a fast thinker. He had to be to keep in Mayer's constant good graces. ''I can kill the newsreels. If the other studios won't cooperate, we refuse to lend them any of our names.''

''Yes! Yes!'' Mayer was rubbing his hands together and practically salivating. ''We'll begin with Zanuck! He wants the hoor Harlow for *In Old Kentucky* — ''

Ida corrected him. *''In Old Chicago.''*

''They changed the title?'' He didn't wait for an answer but plunged on. ''More! More! Give me more trouble we can make!''

Ida was waving her hands at Mayer to calm him down. ''Now just a minute. Slow down. Put on the brakes and let's consider the situation calmly. May I remind both of you that Myrna and Bill know Claire Young, and I don't mean her reputation, but I mean socially.''

Strickling said, ''God knows Powell knows her socially.''

''You should talk,'' snapped Ida. Strickling caught his breath. She said to Mayer, ''You forget Claire spent a lot of time with Myrna preparing her for the call girl in *Penthouse.''*

''Yes, yes, I remember,'' said Mayer. ''But there was no murder then! Now it's murder and it's a scandal what with that lousy little black book of Claire's. Sayyy!'' He was nursing a thought and Ida and Strickling waited until he voiced it. ''Let's make the Claire whoor an offer for the film rights to her little black book!''

Ida rolled her eyes, clasped her hands together, and said, ''And for my next number, ladies and gentlemen, I'd like to sing 'Toot Toot Tootsie, Goodbye.' ''

Mayer raged, ''Ida! You are trying my patience.''

Ida retorted, ''Fair enough. Now try mine.''

Mayer cried, ''Enough! Enough of your insolence!''

Strickling interrupted. ''Listen to me! Herb Villon's in charge of the case. Bill Powell's known him a long time."

Mayer said in a small voice that nevertheless commanded their attention. "Our Herb Villon? The Paul Bern Herb Villon?"

"A very smart gentleman," said Strickling. "I've cultivated his acquaintance over the years. I see that he and his girlfriend are invited to all our premieres."

"Who's his girlfriend?" asked Mayer.

"Why your old buddy Hazel Dickson."

"That *yenta* is his girlfriend? That's the best he can do?"

"Come on now," said Ida, "Hazel's been a friend of the studio for a long time now. She's never let us down, and when we've asked her to help kill a story, she was always on target with her bow and arrow."

Strickling said, "Let me have a talk with Herb. Get him to tell the press he invited Bill and Myrna as observers to help them prepare for the next *Thin Man.*"

With furrowed brows Mayer asked, "What's the next *Thin Man?*"

"The Thin Man's Hernia," suggested Ida.

Mayer glared at her and was thinking, Maybe for Christmas I'll buy her a lover, it might soften her outlook on life and on the other hand the shock might give her a myocardial infarction. He said to Strickling, "Maybe you should go to Claire Young's house and get those two damn fools out of there."

Strickling said, "You could always phone and threaten them."

"Those two? Who could threaten those two? It's as bad as trying to threaten Garbo."

Strickling said, "I don't think it's a good idea for me to show up there."

Mayer bristled. "Why not? Don't you have a house account?"

Ida chuckled. *"Touché,* boss, *touché."*

Mayer stared at the ceiling again, then said, "Okay, Howard. Talk to Herb Villon." He directed his eyes from the ceiling to Strickling. "You sure he won't let us down?"

"He didn't let us down when we turned up with Paul Bern's suicide note."

"Yes. You're right. We took too long finding that suicide note."

"Some suicide note," said Ida. "It certainly wasn't a Pulitzer prize winner."

Mayer wondered if he could draw a suspended sentence for slamming her on the jaw.

At Claire Young's house, everyone had assuaged their hunger with sandwiches, beer, and coffee. Lazlo was at the french windows offering a soulful rendition of "When the Moon Comes Over the Mountain." Freda was watching Myrna, who sat in a chair deep in thought. She hadn't eaten. She was still upset by her Claire Young theory. But somehow, she couldn't shake her intuition that Claire might know more then she was telling. The secret little black book, and now her dictating her memoirs. But there were other secrets she suspected Claire was harboring. Powell came and sat at her feet.

"Where are you, Minnie? I have a feeling you're off in another dimension, one totally alien to Beverly Hills."

Myrna shifted in her seat and smiled at him. "We're practically like *The Corsican Brothers,* aren't we. The separated Siamese twins who continue to share each other's emotions and each other's pains. I'm not off in another dimension. My train of thought is still on the same track, but a bit more sophisticated."

He said firmly as he started to light a cigarette, "Claire didn't kill Fern Arnold."

"I'm convinced you're right. It's geographically impossible if she was dictating to Amelia Hubbard in West Hollywood. Still, Villon should have phoned this Hubbard woman to corroborate Claire's alibi, don't you agree?"

Powell exhaled and then studied the lighted end of the cigarette. "Minnie, although I still believe Claire is innocent of what the newspapers will undoubtedly label a heinous crime, Claire could easily have set up an alibi for herself with Miss Hubbard. I think I heard sonewhere that in an earlier incarnation our Miss Hubbard had been one of Claire's girls."

"Oh dear, there is certainly a plethora of Claire's girls in Hollywood."

Villon joined them. He asked, "Still troubled, Myrna?"

"Well, if you're wishing I would draw a blank on this case, it's not all that easy. I'm just an amateur busybody, of course, but to my naked eye, things don't seem the way they ought to be. Take the poker. The murder weapon. No fingerprints. The handle wiped clean." Villon nodded. Myrna wasn't happy. "This killer has seen too many movies. They're always wiped clean in the movies."

"Am I interrupting a conference?" asked Claire Young, holding a mug of coffee.

"Not at all," said Powell. "Claire, where's the help?"

"I wish I knew. I could certainly use some."

"I mean household help, dear. Don't you have a housekeeper? A butler? Perhaps a bouncer for any fractious patrons."

Claire said, "Bill, let me quote from The Madam's Handbook."

Myrna was wide-eyed. "Is there really such a thing?"

Claire tapped a finger against her head. "It's in here, Myrna. Etched with lightning. First of all, there is no activity on these premises other than to bring a girl and a score together. They go elsewhere *pour le sport,* as the French would say. Although Fern keeps a small apartment of her own in West Hollywood, she rarely uses it except for the occasion when she's been out on the town and is too tired to come back here. We do our own cooking, our own housekeeping, and there's a maid who comes a couple of times a week, today not being one of them. I don't get much in the way of drop-in trade because I don't encourage it. Sometimes the girls come by when they get antsy and I haven't phoned. Oh Christ, how I'm missing Fern already!"

"There there dear," said Myrna, "have you thought of sending for your aunt? You know, the one in Venice."

"Maidie?"

"Do you have any other aunt in Venice?" asked Myrna, wanting to add, Do you have any other anybody? but not asking for fear of landing her foot in her mouth.

Claire said firmly, "I'd never subject Maidie to this ordeal."

"Doesn't she know how you've been earning your living?" asked Myrna.

"No, she doesn't. She thinks I run a model agency."

Maidie, thought Myrna, has got to be blessedly naive, or feebleminded. And Claire doesn't like talking about her or about anybody else. Myrna suspected Claire's brain was a Pandora's box of dark and dangerous secrets, a very complex personality who could shed one identity and then assume another with the snap of a finger. Audrey Manners into Claire Young quicker than Bill could flip a quip to Myrna. But, thought Myrna, I shouldn't be so hard on her. She's dying, her best friend has been murdered right here on the hearth in this very room, and outside of two prostitutes, a mad violinist (who appropriately enough was now scraping away at "Melancholy Baby"), and William Powell and Myrna Loy, no one has materialized rallying to her side.

A detective appeared from the front hall. "Anybody send for a doctor?"

Myrna blushed. Someone has rallied to Claire's side. Dollars to doughnuts, thought Myrna, it's Mitchell Carewe.

Claire seemed taken by surprise as Mitchell Carewe, carrying his black medical bag, came walking past the detective as though he had every right to be here. He went to Claire. "Are you all right? I was at the hospital and just heard the news on my car radio so I sped here as fast as I could. Are you all right?"

"About as all right as I can be when my best friend has been found murdered in this room."

He put his black bag on Claire's desk. "You need a sedative."

"I don't need a thing! Mitch, I don't think you know everyone." She introduced him, although Myrna got the impression she wished the doctor was anywhere but in this room.

As Powell shook the doctor's hand he asked, "How's for a freebie?" and stuck his tongue out.

"Bill!" Myrna admonished.

Carewe laughed and said, "Just like in the movies!"

"Doctor, I think we've met way back when, before last night," said Powell.

"I don't think so. I certainly would have remembered. It's not every day that one meets William Powell and Myrna Loy."

Myrna said quickly, "Oh, we haven't met before. I've seen you, but we've never met. Last night at Griselda's Cage, you were with Fern Arnold." She added slowly, "The victim."

"I've known Fern a long time. Met her the same time I met Claire. I didn't see you at Griselda's."

Myrna said airily, "That's because you were so engrossed with her before she made her sudden exit leaving you in the lurch."

Herb Villon was thinking, Lucky Myrna Loy wasn't around at the time of the Spanish Inquisition. She'd have made Torquemada, the cruel Inquisitor, look like an also-ran. Hazel said to him with mock sweetness, "Who's in charge here?"

"Quiet," said Herb. "She moves in mysterious ways and I approve of all of them."

Dr. Carewe wore a thin smile. "Fern couldn't give me much time. She was meeting somebody."

Pretty lame excuse, thought Villon. He glanced at Claire. Yes, pretty lame, Claire knows better.

Powell said, "As I said before, I think we've met."

"Forgive me, but I repeat, I don't remember."

"It was on the *Deerslayer*." He turned to Herb. "You remember the ship, don't you, Herb?"

"I helped put it out of business."

Powell explained to the room, "It was a gambling ship. Plied its trade outside the five-mile limit. Or was it ten? Anyway, they cleaned out a lot of suckers."

"Including you," said Myrna.

Powell made a mock bow. "Guilty as charged. Actually, it was the former Mrs. Powell, my beloved Carole, who they were taking to the cleaners until that smarty pants accused the bums of using loaded dice. And they were. I was there, Dr. Carewe, when I believe you were getting wiped out at roulette."

Villon was enjoying himself immensely. These movie stars know no shame. They tread where angels fear, and pity the angels who get in their way. They'll get knocked on their backsides with perhaps only their wings to cushion the shocks.

Carewe said bravely, "Well, if you say I was there, then perhaps

I was. But weren't gambling ships a long time ago? Six or seven years ago? I was just getting started. I couldn't have had the money with which to gamble."

"That's right. You didn't. Oh dear. I shouldn't have brought it up. It's one of the many things Mrs. Hornblow and I have in common. We're very rash and impetuous."

"Six or seven years ago," said Carewe, "I wore a mustache. So I don't see how you can remember me."

"That's because you didn't wear a mustache. You look now the way you did then except now you're more uncomfortable and I do apologize if I'm the cause of it. Claire, aren't you going to offer the doctor a drink?"

"Of course," said Claire, wishing for an earthquake that would scatter everyone, "scotch highball, right?" The doctor nodded. Myrna thought, so she knows what he drinks. Do they belt them back in his office?

Freda, all smiles and coquetry, asked the doctor, "Are you hungry? We had sandwiches but they are all gone. I could prepare you an omelet."

Claire said, "I'm sorry. There aren't any eggs."

Doctor Carewe said, "Please don't fuss. A drink is all I need."

I'll bet, thought Myrna.

"There is no fuss. This will be my *spécialité*. A true Hungarian omelet. Lazlo, put aside the fiddle and go steal a dozen eggs."

FIFTEEN

$\mathcal{M}$yrna sat quite still, staring into space. Her head was spinning. Bill remembering Dr. Carewe from a gambling ship. Stealing eggs for an omelet. And now Villon was on the phone speaking to someone he called Howard. Powell caught her attention and mouthed "Strickling." Myrna's mouth formed an O. Into the phone Villon said "Sure" followed by "Of course" and then "Don't worry about it. I'll handle it. I'll keep in touch." He hung up and crossed to Powell and Loy. "That was Howard Strickling." The way both feigned a combination of shock and fear, Villon was convinced they'd been rehearsing the act for years. "Papa Mayer is very unhappy."

Powell asked, "What young actress had the guts to say no?"

"He wishes you'd both get the hell out of here and go memorize a script."

Myrna said, "I hope you told Strickling to tell Mr. Mayer what we do in our own time is none of his business."

Villon said, "Neither gentlemen knew you were here at my invitation to research your next *Thin Man* film. How could you have forgotten to tell them?"

Myrna said, "William Powell, shame on you. Keeping such momentous information from the Hardy Boys of Hollywood. That was quick thinking on your part, Herb. Consider your back patted."

Villon said, "Pat Strickling on the back. It was his idea, not mine."

Powell said to Myrna, "Minnie, what's ailing you?"

"Why?"

"Why? Because I'm concerned. I'm very unhappy if you're very unhappy, remember *The Corsican Brothers*."

"I'm still remembering the *Maine*."

"Now don't be sassy."

"How can I be sassy if I'm out of sorts?"

Powell said, "How out of sorts are you?"

Myrna began to bristle. "I am not out of sorts. I'm not out of anything. Talk to Claire. She's out of eggs."

"No longer," said Powell, as Lazlo crossed the outer hall on his way to the kitchen carrying a paper bag that Powell was sure contained a carton of eggs. Freda had also spotted the musician and hurried after him. Lucy Rockefeller was off in a corner of the room with Jim Mallory, both occupying a love seat and very deep in conversation.

Powell persisted. "Minnie, I'm sure the doctor has something in his little black bag that will steady your nerves. We seem to be up to our shoulders in little black somethings. Little black bag. Little black book. And anyone for *Little Black Sambo*? No? Good. I only remember the title. Dr. Carewe . . ."

Carewe and Claire were seated at the desk, Claire behind it and Carewe next to her. Neither one of them seemed to be enjoying their conversation. Upon hearing Powell call his name, the doctor's head shot around. At the same time the phone rang and Villon, being the closest to it, picked it up.

Powell said to Carewe, "Myrna seems to be in need of a sedative . . ."

"I am not!" insisted Myrna.

"This is no time for modesty. Perhaps you have something in your little black bag . . ."

"The only thing he might have in that bag that I could use is a good script. Do you have a good script in that bag, Doctor?"

Carewe had arisen and was clutching the black bag tightly. "I'm afraid all I'm carrying are the instruments I might need when I'm doing my rounds at the hospital."

"That sounds terribly efficient," said Myrna. "Don't trouble yourself, Doctor. What I need isn't carried in a medical bag. Now Bill, you shut up. Herb is finished with his call and wants to tell us something."

Herb said with a twinkle in his eye, "That was the coroner. I asked him to call as soon as he'd made a preliminary examination of Fern. He's quite pleased with her."

"Oh come on, Herb!" said Hazel.

"A simple fractured skull. The killer had a powerful wallop." Claire crossed to the bar and poured herself a neat scotch. "Our coroner is a rather fey gentleman. One of the old school. He's beside himself that there is no poison involved. I'd go easy on the scotch if I was you, Claire."

"Why?" she snapped, "I've got plenty." Her voice was husky and her hands were trembling.

Hazel said to Villon, "That was unbecoming."

"What are you talking about?"

"Simple fractured skull. Powerful wallop. No poison. Fern Arnold was Claire's closest friend. Claire's hurting bad and you had to make it worse."

Villon spoke softly, "There is method to my madness."

"I think there's madness to your method." She went to Claire. "Mind if I join you?"

"Not at all." Claire made room at the bar for Hazel, who methodically mixed a pitcher of gin martinis.

Powell was watching her and called across the room, "I hope you're mixing enough for a lot of us."

Freda came bustling into the room carrying a tray on which

there was a plate of Hungarian omelet with buttered toast and a small vase with an artificial rose. She crossed to the desk with a lavish smile of pride and self-satisfaction while Hazel assured Powell there'd be plenty of martinis for whoever wanted them. Freda set the tray down on the desk and said to Dr. Carewe, "Eat! Eat! Look how you look. Here it is. My Hungarian omelet, I don't make it for everyone. Here is buttered toast and a fork and a knife and a miserable artificial rose I found on the refrigerator. Doctor? Have you lost your appetite?"

"I didn't have one," he said weakly. "But it looks awfully good."

"Aha!" cried Freda triumphantly, "nobody can resist my omelets."

Powell said in an aside to Myrna, "I'm sure that's a metaphor for something racy."

Myrna said to Villon, who was now standing with them, "Did you realize how hard you were being on Claire?"

"Hazel's already brought it to my attention." He was lighting a cigarette.

Myrna now wore a look of curiosity and Powell could tell she was harboring some interesting ideas. He said, "Come, come, Minnie. Let's have it." She shot him a look. "I can tell by your very expressive face you're struggling with something you want to say but can't make up your mind whether to say it or not."

"It isn't anything I want to say, it's something I want to ask."

Villon said, "Go ahead and ask."

"Herb, I have this nagging feeling that you know who financed Claire."

"And if I say I don't?"

"I'd ask you to swear it on a Bible."

"We don't have a Bible," said Powell. "And nobody's going to send out for one."

"We don't have to send out for one, there's a Bible on that bookshelf. It looks pretty old from here but I'm sure it's still serviceable."

Powell asked, "My dear Minnie, my mind is beginning to boggle. What has Claire's financing got to do with Fern's murder?"

Myrna looked around with caution. Lazlo had resumed his fiddling with "Let's Have Another Cup of Coffee, Let's Have Another Piece of Pie." "We can't be overheard, can we?"

Powell reassured her. "I'm sure we're well out of earshot of the others and Lazlo is bearing down rather heavily on his instrument. I do wish Hazel would stop being so meticulous with her martini measurements. My tongue is beginning to swell."

"Let her take her time. I don't want her in on any of this." She took the precaution of looking around again. "When Claire was Audrey Manners, she had a romance with a young intern. Well, it stands to reason that was Mitchell Carewe."

"I'm sure at the time there was a vast assortment of interns for Miss Manners to select from, and not necessarily Carewe."

Myrna said with patience, "Bill, this is my theory. If it doesn't interest you, go attack Hazel and develop a theory of your own. Now, may I continue? Herb, you have one of those looks on your face germane to detectives. Please bear with me."

Powell asked, "We'll bear with you after you explain that remark about the look on Herb's face being germane to detectives."

"Skepticism," said Myrna.

"Well, can you blame him after the humdingers you've already come up with?"

Myrna chose to ignore the remark. "Dr. Carewe remains my intern of choice because if he isn't, my theory gets knocked into a cocked hat and I wore one of them in *Don Juan* and I thought I looked like hell. You figure in this too, Bill."

"Oh my! Thank you, Minnie, I'm often at my best figuring in things."

"Herb, last night Griselda mentioned that Mitchell Carewe has heavy gambling debts. Well, I think it's a chronic condition with him harking back to the days when he gambled on the *Deerslayer*. I think at some point back then the doctor was terrified for his life. He knew Audrey had a wealthy backer and I think he went to her to get her to intercede with him and get the money he needed to pay his gambling debts. You're not looking so skeptical anymore, Herb."

"Because it's logical. But that is, as Bill isn't so sure, if Carewe is our pigeon."

"Well let's let him be our pigeon until I'm finished. Look at the poor man struggling with that omelet. He's terribly attractive, isn't he?"

Bill said with exaggerated patience, "He's not my type."

"He's not mine either," said Myrna, "but he is terribly attractive even if his eyes are a little too close together."

Herb said, "Get back to your theory, Myrna."

"Where was I? Oh yes, Audrey to get the money from Mr. Moneybags to settle Carewe's debt. Well, I think he refused to give it to her."

"Why?" asked Bill.

"Why not?" piped in Villon.

"I think Mr. Money Bags was an older gentleman. Not much older, but older. I think he was the type of man who had crushes on young blonde starlets."

"Why blondes necessarily?" asked Powell.

"Wasn't Audrey a blonde? Wasn't she, Herb?"

"Yes," said Herb, "she was a blonde."

"Why is the color of her hair so important? She's a brunette now that she's Claire Young."

"Bill, you're being very dense. Herb, all this was at a time when Baby was starting to emerge so successfully as the Platinum Blonde, wasn't it?"

Powell's eyes widened. "Baby? My Baby? My Jean?"

"And just about every starlet in Hollywood bleached her hair blonde to try and get a piece of the action. Right?" Herb said nothing. "And although Paul Bern was married to the biggest blonde star of all, he still treasured a secret passion for Audrey Manners and was jealous of any man she was interested in. And he'd been interested in Audrey for a long time. About when did she become Claire Young and open her business?"

"It was 1927," Herb told her.

"Approximately nine years ago," Myrna added quietly. "You were having your romance with Audrey at the time?"

"It was over by then. Oh boy, Myrna Loy, you sure do know how to open old wounds."

"Oh dear," said a chagrined Myrna, "that's not what I had in mind at all."

Herb said, "It's okay, I was over Audrey a long time ago. About the time I was promoted to detective, Audrey recovered and went into business."

"Recovered?" said Powell. "She was ill?"

"A long time ill," said Herb. "She had a severe nervous breakdown."

"Oh the poor girl. It's all so biblical, like the curses of the pharaoh. How Claire has suffered." Appropriately, Lazlo was sawing away at "Hearts and Flowers." And Hazel was approaching with a tray laden with several glasses filled with gin martinis.

"Damn," said Myrna, "here comes Hazel. It's time for an intermission."

"What's going on with you three?" asked Hazel suspiciously.

"Why Hazel," said Myrna, thinking quickly, "it concerns Christmas gifts and we can't tell you." She took a martini hungrily as did Powell. Hazel took a third and put the tray on an end table.

Powell asked, "No martini for Herb?"

Hazel said, "Detectives can't drink when they're on duty."

"What an awful profession," said Myrna as she savored and reveled in her first sip.

Powell said admonishingly, "Minnie Minnie Minnie. You didn't mean to call Herb's profession an awful one?"

"Yes I did, and from the way he's watching you dive into your martini, I can see he agrees with me. Herb, did you always want to be a cop?"

"No. I didn't want to be a fireman either."

Hazel had a questioning look on her face. "I don't understand myself."

"What's wrong?" asked Myrna.

Hazel said, "You barely know him and already you've found out police work wasn't his first choice of profession. I never asked him that ever!"

"There's a simple explanation for that," said Myrna. "I assume you met him when he was already promoted to detective."

"That's right. Just about then."

"Well then, Hazel," said Myrna, "you probably assumed, and rightly so, that a detective was all he ever wanted to be, just like Herb's probably never questioned if you ever wanted to do anything else besides sell gossip."

"I wanted to be a beautician," said Hazel. "I even went to school. Cost my parents a small fortune. Even today I still get this terrible urge to put my fingers into another woman's hair."

"I hope you don't mean me," said Myrna.

"I don't mean anybody. I just mean women in general. Shall I get the pitcher for refills?"

"Oh yes!" said Myrna gratefully.

"Be right back," said Hazel and hurried to the bar, while the three watched her go.

"Let's get back to the nervous breakdown," said Myrna conspiratorially.

Herb told them, "It was the business with the scandal, the producer who was Audrey's self-styled protector at Metro and his wife demanding that Louis B. Mayer get rid of Audrey as only that bastard could and can. So it was too much for Audrey."

"What about the producer who had a case on Audrey and later financed her? Couldn't he somehow intervene?"

"Too frightened," said Herb.

"Of what?" asked Powell.

"Of some skeletons rattling around in his own closet. Among those was his involvement with an actress who died of a drug overdose."

"Barbara Lamarr?" asked Myrna quickly, Lamarr having been a top Metro star who died of an overdose in 1926.

"Maybe," said Herb. "Well, I might as well open my closet door a few inches. You asked if there wasn't something I wanted to be other than a detective. People, I was born here. I grew up here. I went to school here. I was on a steady diet of Hollywood and movie stars. I wanted to be a movie star."

"You sap," said Powell.

"My father's very words." He paused for a moment and then a sweet smile formed. "I had a screen test at Metro. Audrey tested with me. That's when we began. It didn't last long because my test was a flop and Audrey was moving up."

Myrna said, "You miss Audrey."

"Yes, I miss Audrey," said Herb, "but I'm not all that nuts about Claire Young."

Powell said, "Myrna, you suddenly look dyspeptic. And why, pray tell, is that?"

"Since I don't know what dyspeptic is supposed to look like, I can only tell you that I was at Metro when Barbara Lamarr died, and I might add, Mr. Villon, a supposed suicide which it wasn't, her mentor and protector was Paul Bern."

Powell asked, "Baby's Paul Bern?"

"I can't think of any other Paul Berns," said Myrna smartly. "Herb, it was Paul Bern who financed Audrey Manners into Claire Young, wasn't it. He was sweet on her, wasn't he?"

"Yes. It was Paul Bern. But don't tell Hazel. Paul Bern's dead. Let him rest in peace. He didn't know any in his short lifetime."

"That's very dear, Herb," said Myrna. "At the time of Bern's murder, a woman committed suicide by jumping off the San Francisco ferry. She was identified as a woman Bern had been supporting for a long time. She purportedly had come to see him the day he was killed."

Herb filled in the rest. "We pinned the murder on her with Louis B. Mayer's blessing. Our only other suspect was Miss Harlow."

Bill leapt to his fiancée's defense. "She was spending the night at her mother's."

"Now Bill," said Myrna, "You and I know Baby isn't in any way capable of killing anyone." She said to Villon, "You were on the case, weren't you, Herb?"

"Peripherally. The top muckamucks in the force were running the show. Jim Mallory and I were supporting players, very minor supporting players."

Powell said, "Louis B. Mayer and Howard Strickling were running the show, and everybody in this Godforsaken town knows it." He smiled at Herb Villon. "Let's not kid ourselves. That was a very corrupt police force back then." Herb Villon reserved comment.

"Oh my," said Myrna. "So it's possible this woman who jumped off the ferry turned into a convenience for the police. Paul Bern's killer might still be at large. And if so, Herb, my theory that his murder might have a link to Fern's bears examining."

Herb didn't answer her. Detective Zachary Forrest was hurrying into the room. "Herb! I just checked in with the precinct. There's been another murder. Some woman named Amelia Hubbard."

SIXTEEN

$\mathcal{A}$melia Hubbard!" exclaimed Myrna.

"What about Amelia?" asked Claire.

Zachary Forrest looked perplexed. He had no way of knowing Claire had been Amelia's friend. Villon quickly explained to Forrest, who then said to Claire, "Sorry, Miss Young."

Claire was walking slowly toward the two detectives. Jim Mallory abandoned Lucy Rockefeller to hear the rest about Amelia Hubbard. Freda watched Mitchell Carewe as he slowly followed Claire, arms outstretched as though he expected her to faint and fall back into his arms. "Herb? What's happened to Amelia?"

"She's been found dead." Claire's hand flew to her mouth to stifle a scream. "She was murdered." He asked Forrest, "Let's have it all."

"In front of everybody?" asked Forrest.

"Why? You got stage fright?"

"Hell, no. Some kid found her. A messenger. He was bringing her some stuff to type. Her door was slightly ajar. He rang her bell and then called her name. The way he told it, he decided she might have gone out and forgotten to lock her door. So he thought he'd go in and leave the envelope where she'd spot it. This is what he told Barney Hoyt."

"Barney's on the case?" Forrest told Myrna and Powell, "Barney's good. He's very good."

"I like Barney," said Myrna.

"You've met Barney Hoyt?" asked Powell, slightly bemused.

"Oh no. But I love his name. It's so he-mannish."

Villon said, "He's very short."

"Oh dear," said Myrna sadly, "another illusion shattered."

Forrest was saying to Villon, "So the kid goes into the apartment and what he sees nauseates him. A woman seated at her typewriter, her body slumped forward, a wound in her neck."

"This is a bad day for womanhood," said Myrna, eyeing Mitchell Carewe with his arms around Claire, who was sobbing into his chest. Powell told her to hush up.

Forrest continued. "The kid, you know, the messenger, he got the building superintendent. The super took one look at the woman and phoned for the cops." He coughed and then said, "Barney wants you and Jim there. He knows she connects to Fern Arnold's murder — " he lowered his voice — "and to Claire Young."

"By all means Jim and I are going there."

"Oh, we wouldn't miss this for the world!" chirped Myrna.

"We may have to," said Powell. "We haven't been asked to join the gentlemen."

Myrna faced Villon. "Now really, Herb, you can't exclude us now. We've been so helpful. Well, haven't we?"

Villon asked Forrest for Amelia's address. Then he instructed Forrest to let the precinct know he and Mallory were leaving for the scene of the latest crime, but refrained from adding he had little stomach for it. For the moment, he didn't share with anyone his feelings that outside of the murderer, Claire Young was probably the last person to see Amelia Hubbard alive. He didn't have to share it with Myrna, who sotto voce had just expressed the same sentiment to Bill Powell. Powell nodded in agreement and then looked at Claire in Dr. Carewe's arms. She looked and sounded sincere. In fact, at this moment, she was the very pathetic picture of an emotional wreck. Hazel Dickson was saying to Claire sympathetically, "There there, dear, there there." No one seemed to have noticed that she had already phoned Louella but spoke to Louella's equally vicious assistant, Dorothy Manners, and that she was anxious to get to the scene of the crime.

Villon addressed the assemblage in the room, as Lazlo softly played "Auld Lang Syne." Freda stood with Lucy Rockefeller, who had just told her she could go for Jim Mallory and warned Freda not to scoff. Freda chose not to scoff; she sneered. Her mind was on Amelia Hubbard, Fern Arnold, and Claire Young. But her ears heard Villon telling them not to leave the premises and promising to be back as soon as possible.

Dr. Carewe remonstrated, "I have appointments."

"Cancel them," said Villon, "you know where the phone is. Come on, Jim, let's get going."

Myrna grabbed Powell's hand and pulled him after her. Hazel gave Claire a farewell pat on the shoulder and hurried out. Claire raised her head and then pulled away from Carewe. The look on Claire's face alerted Freda, who crossed to her, put her arm around her, and guided her to the bar where she knew the liquid solace would be dependable.

Suddenly Claire gasped. She ran after Villon, who was out front instructing his team to be sure no one left the house until he returned and dismissed them. Claire came running out the door crying his name. He went to meet her.

"What's wrong?"

She told him about the many pages she had dictated to Amelia. Earlier material already typewritten was on the top shelf of Amelia's living room closet. And there was her stenographic pad, what she had dictated that morning. Amelia couldn't possibly have had the time to type up the morning work. Villon reassured her he'd protect the material, if it was still there. Claire's heart sank. *If it was still there.* She watched him go to the unmarked car where Jim Mallory was already positioned behind the wheel. He dreaded being Villon's passenger. Mallory agreed with Hazel that Villon drove like the proverbial little old lady from Pasadena. Powell and Hazel were revving their respective motors, Powell with misgivings that he shared with Myrna.

"Minnie, as Dash Hammett I'm sure would agree, this plot is beginning to thicken much too dangerously for my taste."

Myrna said huffily, "William Powell, you know I will never condone or forgive an act of cowardice."

"Mine is not an act of cowardice, mine is an act of common sense. We're actors, not detectives. And on this rare occasion I heartily concur with that archfiend Mayer: we should be somewhere memorizing our scripts."

"I've memorized mine and I wish I could forget it. *Double Wedding* is triple hooey."

"Although ephemeral, I find it rather amusing and we shall be wonderful in it."

"Why not? We've played it before and will play it again. I can assure you, Mr. Powell, under the sign of Metro's Leo the Lion we will never tackle any roles of dramatic substance and I'm not walking out on Herb Villon."

"Supposing he invites you to walk out!"

"I'll take one of Claire's pokers and bash your skull."

"Why, Minnie, I had no idea you had a homicidal bone in your body."

"Never mind my body, don't you dare suggest to Herb Villon that he give us our walking papers. Damn it, this is the first time in years I've done anything constructive. I really mean that. And I know Herb Villon appreciates some of our ideas."

"*Our* ideas? They're mostly *your* ideas." He had lit a cigarette and rolled down his window to let the smoke escape. "Want a puff?"

"No, I don't." She thought for a moment and then said, "Barbara Lamarr had jet black hair."

"So what?"

"She was no blonde like Baby and Audrey Manners."

"But she was absolutely stunning. I had a crush on her."

"You didn't say you knew her!"

"Just in passing. I used to see her at the occasional party or in a restaurant." He paused. "I think Paul Bern kept her supplied with the stuff that killed her. She was an absolute wreck when she died. I was told there was little trace of her great beauty. Okay, Minnie, who do you suspect killed Paul Bern?"

"The same person who killed Fern Arnold and Amelia Hubbard."

"Minnie, are you trying to set yourself up the way Claire Young has supposedly set herself up?"

"Bill, look at Bern's death sensibly. We know Mayer and Strickling rearranged the whole suicide scene when they found the note that Bern had written to Baby days *before* the suicide."

"No, I did not know that and that's the truth."

"Baby told me herself. She didn't tell you?"

"No." He sounded and looked glum.

"Well, don't you go getting mad at her. She told me he wrote the note the morning after a knock-down-drag-out they had. The note was still in her dresser drawer where Strickling found it and convinced Mayer it would be perfect as a suicide note." She quoted: " 'P.S. You realize last night was just a comedy' or something like that. You ninny, don't you realize those two monsters were convinced Baby had shot Bern? Oh Bill, don't look like that."

"How do I look?" he asked glumly.

"Suave and urbane like Philo Vance."

"There isn't a camera trained on me."

"My eyes are trained on you and I'm as good as a camera. Stop brooding about Baby. There's no way she could have murdered Paul Bern."

"Be realistic. Her only alibi was her mother and stepfather and she was and still is their meal ticket. They'd lie through their false teeth to protect her."

"How do you know their teeth are false? You're being mean, and that's very unlike you."

"She told me when they're available she uses Mario's to crack walnuts."

Myrna was looking through the windshield at the familiar sights of her childhood and then forced herself back to Jean Harlow. "Baby swore to me she did not kill Paul Bern. Jean Harlow was my first friend when I rejoined Metro. She was the only actress on the lot who didn't feel threatened even though they had me wear a blonde wig in *The Wet Parade*. I looked ridiculous. Stop thinking about Baby as a possible murderer and worry about her health. I spoke to my doctor this morning and mentioned her sallow skin and how the sparkle's gone out of her eyes and he said it could be renal-oriented, meaning her kidneys. Christian Science or no Christian Science you get her to my doctor when she gets back from Catalina. Now stop that, Bill, Baby's going to be just fine."

"She has to be. She's my world."

"Oh Bill. How sweet. Now Bill, you realize Claire Young could very well be the last person to have seen Amelia Hubbard alive."

"Or dead."

"Congratulations."

"Why kill a woman to whom she's been giving dictation? Presumably very intimate, and for some, very damaging dictation."

"Spoilsport."

"Minnie, Claire Young is a genuinely frightened lady. She has triggered an event that has led to the murder of two people she cared about. I assume she cared about Amelia Hubbard because her sobs were heart-rending."

"I think her sobs were for the possibility of what she dictated having fallen into very dangerous hands."

"There's that too."

"It's possible she spilled the beans about her affairs with Mitchell Carewe and Herb Villon." Powell agreed. Myrna continued, "We know Herb's not the murderer. He has very strong alibis."

"Now really, Minnie."

"Now really yourself. A good detective has to cover all possibilities. No stone unturned. No string untied."

"And no mother to guide her."

"Bill Powell, this is no time for non sequiturs."

"I was thinking of Claire. No mother to guide her. No one to turn to except that overpowering Hungarian and all she's interested in is inheriting the business from Claire. I overheard her."

"I hope she does. I think she'd make a marvelous madam."

"How many madams have you known?

Myrna chose not to answer, and instead said, "What about this Maidie person out in Venice?"

"Aunt Maidie?" Powell thought for a moment. "What about her? She's just an aunt."

Myrna suggested slyly, "She could possibly be her mother."

"Why not?" asked Powell affably. "Every girl should have a mother unless she's too poor to afford one. I must say, Minnie, that mind of yours does go off on tangents. How could she possibly be her mother?"

"Claire is so devious. First Audrey Manners. Then Claire Young. Then that damned little black book. And her memoirs. She's desperate for money. Who for? Aunt Maidie?"

"Why not? I'm sure she adores Aunt Maidie. Claire's scenario could go something like this. She's orphaned as a child."

"I'm stifling a sob," said Myrna.

"Aunt Maidie provides a home for her. Sends her to school. Clothes and feeds her. Teaches her the facts of life. Encourages her to become an actress — "

Myrna took over. "While sitting at home and sewing a scarlet A to the front of her dresses. Dear old Aunt Maidie. Such a comfort. Well, aunt or mother, Claire Young has got to have a deeper reason to accumulate the sum of cash I feel quite safe in assuming she's after."

He stared at her for a moment before concentrating on the traffic ahead of him. "Come come, Minnie. Out with it. The suspense is killing me. What manner of outrage are you entertaining now?"

"It's not an outrage, it's a logical suspicion."

"All your suspicions are certainly logical."

She said with indignation, "You're damn right they're logical. They may be slightly off center but you have to admit they're logical."

"Come on, Minnie, stop stalling."

"I'm thinking of the desert."

"Okay, so we're in Palm Springs. Rather warm for Christmas, don't you think?"

"Presumably where Claire went with her nervous breakdown. Well, Hollywood ladies go to Palm Springs for other reasons and I'm not talking about suntans or not-so-innocent flirtations with tennis pros."

Powell said, "Well, what cuisine I've eaten when there has never been terribly exceptional. So they wouldn't drive out there especially for a meal."

"You're being intentionally dense. Think of Constance Bennett, Miriam Hopkins, Loretta Young."

"I love thinking about them. They're so beautiful and sexy, although Connie is a bitch and Miriam is a pain in the ass and Loretta is so holier-than-thou you'd think she was sired by a priest. All right, now that you've got me on track, what about your sister stars?"

"After a very long absence, they all returned to Hollywood with a babe-in-arms they claimed they had adopted."

"Oh fie and for shame!"

"And they didn't leave them on anybody's doorstep either. They just continued to live the lie. I must ask Clark if he still insists Loretta's daughter isn't his. The child's protruding ears are a dead giveaway."

"Perhaps the child's protruding ears are simply protruding ears."

"I think Claire Young, while still her earlier self, Audrey Manners, betook herself to Palm Springs and there a little child was born. And not in a manger."

"Why Mrs. Arthur Hornblow, Jr., you do come up with some lulus!"

"Well? It's possible, isn't it?"

"Oh yes, it is most certainly possible. In this town illegitimate children are epidemic. I wouldn't be a bit surprised if there were some of mine sitting in lawyer's offices right now preparing lawsuits."

Myrna laughed. "Oh Bill, how could you possibly have fathered an illegitimate child?"

He said casually, "The usual way. Unless I've missed out on an alternative."

"Now don't be frivolous!"

"I'm not in the least bit frivolous. I'm not the frivolous type. You could be right. Now clutched to Aunt Maidie's protective bosom is a little bastard who calls Claire Mommy. And so Claire needs money to see that the child is well provided for. Minnie," he said after a pause in which he further weighed the possibility of their supposition, "it's a likelihood. But even if it is, it doesn't give us a clue as to who murdered three people."

Myrna said, "Mallory and Hazel are pulling in ahead of us."

"My eyesight's quite good. I see them. I see also several police cars. A variety of reporters and camera men. Some nosy neighbors. An ambulance, which means the body has not yet been removed. Oh goody." He pulled in behind Hazel Dickson's car. Hazel was on the sidewalk waiting for them. She opened the door on Myrna's side and leaned in. "I was thinking I'd run interference for you two."

Powell said, "Thank you, my dear, but we're old hands at handling the press."

"Oh my God," said Myrna.

"Now what?" asked Powell.

"First Claire's house, now Amelia Hubbard's apartment. Mr. Mayer may have a stroke."

"What a lovely thought, Minnie. You must hold on to it. Brace yourself. Here comes the gaggle of geese."

The press were having a field day, peppering the stars with questions while the newsreel cameras rolled and photographers snapped photos. A few of Amelia Hubbard's neighbors approached the stars for autographs and the two old pros acquiesced affably although Powell loathed to give autographs. He expressed the fear once that there were larcenous ones who would try to trace his signature onto blank checks.

A sob sister shouted to Hazel, "You better share some of the items you get with us or I'll reveal the shame of your birth!"

Hazel shouted back, "You're certainly old enough to have been there!"

Myrna asked Hazel, "Dear, were you born in Palm Springs?"

Hazel rejoined, "Why would I do a thing like that?"

In Amelia Hubbard's apartment, Barney Hoyt was conferring with Herb Villon and Jim Mallory when Myrna, Bill, and Hazel entered. Amelia Hubbard was no longer at her desk. Two of the coroner's men had moved her to a stretcher where they had wrapped her in a sheet.

Myrna squeaked, "I can't look. It's too awful."

"Now Minnie dear," said Powell, "I'm sure you've seen a fair share of bloodied corpses in the course of your career."

"Of course I have. But they were mostly extras and bit players."

"There were also some notable supporting players. Remember that frightful Frenchwoman who had won the Johnny Weissmuller look-alike contest?"

"I could use a martini, right now," said Myrna, knowing full well none would materialize. Villon introduced Powell and Loy to Barney Hoyt, who was indeed short in height, and who immediately began questioning the presence of movie stars at the scene of the crime.

"It's okay, Barney," Villon reassured Hoyt, "they're researching their next *Thin Man* movie."

"Oh yeah?" said Barney Hoyt. "What's it called?"

Powell said pleasantly, *"The Thin Man Goes to Palm Springs."*

Myrna moved to kick him in the shins but Powell spryly sidestepped. Villon was wondering what they were up to, what was with Palm Springs all of a sudden.

Villon asked Barney Hoyt, "There should be a stenographer's pad on her desk." It was Hazel who found it.

Hazel asked, "Is this thing important?"

Villon snatched it from her. "It contains Claire Young's dictation."

Hazel snatched it back. "I can read shorthand." She opened the pad and flipped several pages. She stopped at one, read the column, and with a cry of delight yelled, "Louella will *plotz* when she hears this!"

Villon beat her to the phone and held it behind his back. "The cops first, Hazel, and then maybe Louella. Now take a seat — not at the desk, the blood's not dried yet — " Myrna grimaced. "Open the pad, and read to me. You know how I love being read to."

"I know," said Hazel, "but this isn't pornographic." The stern look on his face told Hazel to sit and read. She sat and flipped open the pad. "Well, this bit here seems very innocuous. It's about a little boy. Seems the poor kid's got polio."

"How awful," said Myrna. "Hazel? Does it say if he lives out in Venice?"

"Say! Are you a mind reader or something? He lives out in Venice with somebody named Maidie Casson. Myrna, do you know her?"

"Never met her. But I know her. Don't we, Bill?"

SEVENTEEN

$\mathcal{P}$owell spoke with exaggerated enunciation, reminding Myrna that she longed to play Eliza in Bernard Shaw's *Pygmalion* but if it ever came to the screen the part would go to Mae West. "Herb, did Audrey Manners have an Aunt Maidie who lived in Venice? Or to couch it slightly differently, does Claire Young have an Aunt Maidie living in Venice?"

Villon cut through the gristle and got to the meat. "You think that's Claire's kid?"

Powell looked at Myrna, who rewarded him with a blank look, much like Greta Garbo's in the final frames of *Queen Christina.* She was not about to commit herself to the status of a small crippled boy who was undoubtedly a bastard but like every small crippled boy, absolutely adorable. Powell finally spoke. "It has to be somebody's kid."

Villon repeated his question. "You think that's Claire's kid?"

"Well, what if it is?" intervened Hazel. "There's lots of illegitimate kids on the loose in this town. God knows how many could be laid at John Barrymore's feet. And Charlie Chaplin, let us not forget."

Powell asked Villon, "Why not ask Claire?"

The coroner, after ordering his assistants to carry their grisly burden out to what he unceremoniously referred to as the meat wagon, intervened to announce to Villon, "She was murdered with a sharp pointed instrument. Right in the back of the neck." He illustrated his statement by poking Hazel in the back of the neck. Hazel yelped while Myrna asked, "You mean something like a knitting needle?"

The coroner smiled at her. "You're Myrna Loy."

"Are you asking or accusing?"

"I'm asking and you're adorable. If I was twenty years younger I'd wrestle you to the floor." His eyes twinkled and Myrna resisted an urge to pinch his cheek. He looked like the popular character actor Etienne Girardot, short, slender, and sixtyish. "No, Miss Loy, not a knitting needle. You would use that to poke out an eye or injure an eardrum," he said as he rocked back and forth on his heels.

"Or knit a sweater," added Powell with his ever-present common sense.

The coroner persisted. "The knitting needle doesn't get my vote. No, not ever."

"How's for a steak knife?" asked Powell.

"Actually, I've been thinking in terms of something like a dentist's pick."

"Don't they have a small curve at the tip?" asked Villon. He had said something to Jim Mallory, who was carrying a chair to the closet.

"There are several dental instruments that are totally devoid of curves. They are straight and if used incorrectly can be deadly. Miss Hubbard's wound was traumatic. I would say that the attack so stunned her it brought on a heart attack."

The room heard Myrna say, "I'm skipping dinner tonight."

Jim Mallory was standing on the chair feeling around in the top shelf of the closet. He got down from the chair, crossed to Villon and told him, "They're gone." Powell and Loy overheard and realized it had something to do with Claire's chasing after Villon and buttonholing him in front of her house as they were leaving for Amelia Hubbard's.

"What's gone?" asked Hazel in her usual forthright manner of treading where angels might fear and causing Villon's rear end to ache.

Myrna volunteered, "I suspect it's pages of Claire's dictation that Amelia typed and consigned to the top shelf of the closet."

"How'd you know that?" asked Villon sharply.

Myrna said staunchly, "I wasn't imparting knowledge, I was sharing a deduction. And I'll stand by what I said. People always hide things on the top shelves of closets. I always do but the trouble is I always forget what I hid and what's worse, why?"

"You must do an inventory of your top shelves at the earliest possible convenience, Minnie — you may find something of value."

Hazel persisted at Villon. "Myrna's right, isn't she."

Villon knew when he was beaten. "Myrna is right."

Myrna smiled victoriously. "So the murderer came here to get those pages, right? He demanded them from Miss Hubbard, whose loyalty overcame what I suppose was her common sense and she said something to the effect that he could not have them and that was that. So he stabbed her with the sharp instrument and set about to find the papers and promptly found them because he probably knows all about people hiding things on the top shelves of their closets."

Powell, who had been carefully scrutinizing the contents of the room, said, "One look at this place and the only logical hiding place is the closet. And Minnie?"

"Yes?"

"What sharp instrument?" Her face was blank again so he elucidated. "You said he stabbed her with a sharp instrument."

"I didn't." She indicated the coroner, who was wishing he had taken his father's advice and become a race track tout. "This adorable darling did."

"Oh, never mind," said Powell, conceding defeat. He asked Villon, "He could have arrived with the weapon concealed on his person. Mr. Hoyt, I presume you didn't find a bloodstained pointed instrument?"

"If I had," replied Barney Hoyt, "we'd be having no problem with the damned thing."

"A very sagaciously practical answer. So Herb, there's a murderer on the loose with a sharp-pointed bloodstained instrument. Do you suppose he's the same person who murdered Fern Arnold?"

"Bill," replied Villon wearily, "it stands to reason."

"We think he also murdered Paul Bern, don't we, Bill," said Myrna.

Powell said, trying to assuage the strange look on Herb Villon's face, "It's only a supposition."

"If he killed Paul Bern," said Villon, "he's a long time between murders."

Myrna asked, "Don't murderers take sabbaticals?" The statement was ignored.

Mallory had been to the kitchen but reported to Villon he'd found no sign of a murder weapon there. Villon told him he didn't think there would be. Villon was at the desk staring at a phone number penciled on Amelia's desk calendar. He dialed the number. An efficient female voice trumpeted, "Dr. Carewe's office." Villon replaced the phone in its cradle. He was wondering, Was Hubbard also a patient of Carewe's, and if so, how could she afford him — he was very high priced. Perhaps Carewe was treating her out of friendship, but treating her for what? Or maybe Hubbard had called him to see if Claire was truly fatally ill. Doctors aren't supposed to share privileged information. Yet perhaps if he and Amelia were buddies from a long way back, he'd have let her in on the diagnosis. And it was a likelihood that Hubbard knew Carewe when they were younger and Carewe was pursuing Audrey Manners.

"Your cheeks are puffed up," Hazel said to Villon.

"They always puff up when I'm thinking."

"They're more puffed up than usual. They look like you've got the mumps." She recognized the expression on Villon's face. It warned her to back off for the moment, but Hazel wasn't one who easily shifted to reverse. "What was that number you just dialed?"

Villon knew that wishing for lightning to strike Hazel was futile. Hazel led a charmed life. In fact she led several charmed lives in addition to her own. Myrna was still wondering if indeed murderers did on occasion take sabbaticals. She remembered reading somewhere about a series of prostitute murders in Los Angeles where the murderer had gone undetected. Then years passed and suddenly prostitutes were being murdered again. It seems there was always open season on ladies of easy virtue, but in this case the fresh murders erupted after a decade's hiatus and Myrna remembered thinking at the time she'd read the article the killer probably had become bored with retirement as happened to most people in retirement (she had read that statistic too somewhere) and had decided it was high old time to get back to murdering whores.

Bill Powell was wondering, How does a murderer walk away with a bloodstained instrument? Wrapped in a newspaper? Certainly not tucked in an inside jacket pocket. There'd be telltale stains. He watched a forensics team give the room a thorough going over. He admired them. They were good. They were very very good. Not much chatter either, just almost total concentration on the job at hand.

Hazel was aching to dial the number Villon had dialed but he had torn the page on which it was written from the desk pad and stuffed it in his pocket. On that page was also a notation signifying that Claire Young was expected at ten that morning. There was a sheet of typing paper rolled up in the carriage of the machine so that it looked totally blank. Villon rolled the carriage. He stared at the paper then tore it out of the machine, folded it, and put in a jacket picket.

"What was that?" asked Hazel.

"A sheet of paper," said Villon.

"What was written on it?"

"Nothing. It was blank."

"Oh yes? Then why fold it and put it in your pocket?"

Powell was within earshot. There was so much about Hazel Dickson that reminded him of his ex-wife. Carole Lombard had always strafed him with suspicious questions. Where were you? What did you do? Why did you do it if you did it? How often had he wanted to wring Lombard's neck and now entertained the same desire for Hazel Dickson. He heard Myrna saying, "I wish there was a butler in this case so we could blame the whole shooting match on him."

"Nobody's been shot in this case," Powell reminded her but she wasn't listening. She was off somewhere else, because a thought that had been nagging at her earlier at Claire's house had resurfaced from her subconscious and was nagging again. "You're not listening to me, Minnie." She was muttering something, completely unaware of what she was saying. "Why Minnie," said an astonished Powell, "what's wrong?"

"What? What?"

"I asked you what's wrong?"

Myrna was bewildered. "What's wrong with what?"

Powell made no effort to mask his exasperation. "You were reciting the Lord's Prayer."

"I was not!"

"You were too! 'Our Father, who art in heaven, hallowed be Thy name . . .' "

"The Bible," said Myrna.

"What Bible? The King James Version?"

"Claire's Bible."

Powell's hands were on his hips. "Okay. I'll bite. What about Claire's Bible?"

"It's out of place on the shelf."

"I see. Well actually I don't. You're not making sense."

She seemed to be making sense to Villon. He had overheard and joined them, hoping to shake his human barnacle, Hazel Dickson, who was not easily shaken. She dogged his footsteps, determined to ferret out the secret information she was positive he was withholding from her.

"It's a very old Bible. One of those old oversized ones I sometimes see on sale in secondhand book stores. Bill, don't you own a Bible?"

"As a matter of fact I do. It's quite a beautiful one and I'm sure quite expensive though I've never had it appraised. It was a gift from Carole's mother that first Christmas she forgave me for marrying her daughter. In fact, I occasionally dip into it when there's little else in the house for me to read. It's rather racy in spots, you know."

"Bill, where do you keep your Bible?"

"When last I saw it it was in my bedroom."

"Standing up between bookends?"

"I don't have bookends in my bedroom. I disapprove of them."

"Isn't your Bible in a drawer?"

"When were you in my bedroom?"

"I've never been in your bedroom." She insisted, "Your Bible is in a drawer, isn't it?"

"If you insist."

"I'm not insisting, I want to know. There's a reason I want to know."

Villon said, "My Bible is in a drawer."

"That's right," corroborated Hazel. "It's in the drawer where he keeps his underwear and his spare revolver. I saw it there."

Myrna knew she was suddenly blushing and refused to try to understand why. Whether it was Hazel's knowledge of the location of Villon's Bible or the presence of Villon's underwear.

Powell said, "I'm standing by you, Herb. Yes, Myrna, my Bible is in a drawer. The one in my night table. Along with an old issue of *Captain Billy's Whiz Bang*." He asked the others in the room, "Any more Bibles to contribute? Miss Loy seems to be on a Bible binge."

The coroner piped up. "Miss Loy seems to have many fine nobilities. Miss Loy, where do you keep your Bible."

"Oh." She was nonplused. "My Bible. Well. I don't own a Bible."

"Tsk," tsked Powell.

"But I'm buying myself one for Christmas. And it's not going to be placed on a bookshelf standing up. It shall be laid reverently in a drawer — "

"With your underwear." Powell had lighted a cigarette and blew a perfect smoke ring which he hoped would settle around the unique tip of Myrna's nose.

The coroner was back again. "Miss Loy, I teach a Bible class every Sunday." He named the church. "I'd be so honored if you'd attend some Sunday soon."

"How sweet of you to ask. I'll discuss it with my publicist. I really think we should be getting back to Claire's. I'm sure the news of Amelia Hubbard's murder has been on the radio by now and someone has probably blabbed to Howard Strickling that Bill and I are at the scene of another crime and dear Louis is undoubtedly flat on his back on the floor of his office in a dead faint, the bluffer. Herb, are you aware there's an informer in your police force? How else could Howard Strickling be privy to our whereabouts so quickly? Unless you're the blabbermouth, Hazel."

"I only blabber for financial rewards," said Hazel, "and Howard Strickling isn't very liberal with financial rewards unless Metro is paying for a cover-up, like they've been very sub rosa waving a pickle under Claire's nose for the right to purchase her little black book."

"Where'd you hear that?" asked Villon.

Hazel countered swiftly. "What was that number you dialed? What's on that sheet of paper you pulled from the typewriter?"

"Hazel," said Villon through clenched teeth, "you should be a matron in a women's jail."

"Or at any rate," Powell whispered to Myrna, "someplace behind bars. I'm beginning to see where Hazel can be very dangerous."

Barney Hoyt was assuring Villon he'd have the forensic results as soon as they were collated and studied although Villon had little hope that the team would come up with anything very useful. Villon promised to keep Barney apprised of any fresh developments from his group.

Hazel had taken Jim Mallory to one side and asked him, "How much info do you share with the waitress?"

Jim played dumb. "What waitress?"

"In the Metro executive dining room."

"Regan?"

"There you go. I've struck a chord."

"Regan isn't interested in information," he lied. "She likes to watch autopsies."

"Before or after lunch?" Hazel continued, "I won't snitch to Herb. You're looking very uncomfortable, Jim."

"Your question is very disturbing."

"It was meant to be."

"One doesn't hold very deep conversations with Regan. One just stalls for time until she says yes or no."

"I don't think she knows how to say no."

"Thank God."

That made Hazel smile. She went to the desk because an idea had struck her. She examined the page on the desk calendar, the one under the page Herb had torn off and pocketed. Amelia had pressed down heavily writing what she had written on the page Herb had in his pocket. With her back to the others Hazel surreptitiously took a pencil from a jar that held an array of them and rubbed the lead quickly over the indentations. A phone number appeared. Claire copied it into her notebook, which she had quietly extracted from her handbag. The other indentation told her of Claire's ten A.M. appointment. She was satisfied, but not totally. She had to know what was on the sheet of paper Villon had pulled from the typewriter.

Myrna said to Powell sotto voce, "Look at Hazel."

"Why? Is she doing card tricks?"

"She's looking very smugly self-satisfied."

Powell said, "As a matter of fact, so are you. What has Minnie's nimble brain come up with now?"

"I'll tell you later."

"Why not now?"

"Because it's purely circumstantial."

"What is?"

"How the murderer got the weapon out of here." She caught herself. "Oh damn! Damn damn damn."

"Don't be mad, Minnie. I still can't cotton to what you're getting at with all these Bibles."

"Not all these Bibles, Bill, just one."

"The one at Claire's place." Myrna said nothing. She turned away from him with a sniff. "Minnie, you're vexing me. I don't like being vexed. We're pals. We're buddies. And for very good salaries, we are on occasion Nick and Nora Charles."

"Well, we aren't now. We're Minnie and Mickey."

"Heavens! I thought we were Myrna and Bill."

"We are! Stop getting me flustered. When I'm flustered I say all the wrong things and think all the wrong things and I think the sooner we get back to Claire's the better."

Villon had heard Myrna and when Powell asked "Why?" Villon said, "Because all the answers are there. Let's get a move on."

EIGHTEEN

$\mathcal{A}$t Claire's Lazlo was dispiritedly rendering his own arrangement of Rodgers and Hart's "Love Me Tonight" and "Lover" because there came a time in every fiddler's life when he wondered what the future held in store for him. He had heard Freda negotiating with Claire to acquire the rights to her business, which consisted mainly of names, addresses, and unlisted phone numbers. Claire conducted the negotiation listlessly, without enthusiasm, and gave Lazlo the impression she wished she was somewhere else. It sounded to him as though Freda was getting the best of the deal and Claire looked to him like she didn't give a damn.

Lucy Rockefeller was wondering why Freda wasn't insisting that the little black book be included in the deal, or maybe it was a tacit understanding that it would be. She hadn't heard either negotiator mention the item. Dr. Carewe had commandeered the telephone and was giving detailed instructions to his nurse and then to his receptionist. Class, she said to herself, he's got real class. So distinguished-looking, with the gray highlighting his temples. He spoke with such calm and self-assurance when he was telling one of his ladies, presumably his nurse, that the next morning he would be occupied at the hospital supervising the amputation of the leg of a diabetic patient. He was so persuasive in his delivery that Lucy was almost hypnotized into volunteering an appendage of her own for radical surgery. And then, as her favorite song said, her heart stood still. Jim Mallory had entered the room followed by Villon, Hazel, and then Powell and Myrna. Lucy looked at Jim and discarded any further thoughts of a romantic liaison with Mitchell Carewe. Villon acknowledged Zachary Forrest who sat quietly at the bar.

In a sense Claire's heart also stood still. She saw what Hazel was holding. Amelia's stenographic pad. They had heard about Amelia's murder on Claire's console Philco radio but the newscaster had told them very little. The coroner's report had not been released, so they had no idea as to how Amelia was killed or why. Claire realized Villon was talking to her. "I'm sorry, Herb," she said, "would you tell me that again?"

"Amelia's been taken to the morgue for an autopsy." He not only had Claire's attention but everyone else's. Powell and Loy had stationed themselves at the bar where Powell lost no time reactivating the pitcher which had held gin martinis. They did not talk to each other, but preferred listening to Herb. Myrna studied faces for reactions. She heard Villon saying, "She was stabbed in the back of the neck with what the coroner says was a long, very sharp instrument, probably surgical in origin. Maybe a dentist's pick. The blow was so powerful, the coroner thinks it might have induced a heart attack."

Lucy emitted a squeal.

Claire questioned Villon under her breath, "The pages?"

"Gone."

Claire paled. Villon feared she was on the verge of fainting. He could never deal with a swooning woman. Hazel had never fainted in all the years she had courted him, she had only passed out from all the booze she frequently imbibed. But Hazel was easy. All he had to do with her was sling her over a shoulder as firemen did with smoke victims and transport her home. Villon said to Claire, "Don't pass out on me." She had grabbed his hand to steady herself. He ordered Jim to bring Claire a brandy. Myrna poured the brandy into a snifter and brought it to Mallory, who handed it to Villon, who pressed the snifter to Claire's lips.

Powell was moving a vermouth bottle back and forth over the pitcher of gin. This was a new one on Myrna. "Is this some form of ritual you've heard about, Bill?"

"Actually, yes. It was taught to me by W. C. Fields. No need to disturb the gin by pouring in the vermouth. Just wave the vermouth bottle back and forth over the pitcher and it will soon dizzy the gin and then *voilà*, you have a perfectly swell martini."

Myrna added wryly, "Inducing a perfectly swell hangover."

"We should swallow a spoonful of sweet butter to coat our stomachs — that'll make us less hangover prone."

"It'll make me fat and I'm not about to go to the kitchen in search of sweet butter. I don't want to miss a thing going on in here. For instance, Claire looks faint."

"Probably heard the papers are missing from the top shelf of Amelia's living room closet."

"Hazel's not helping much by fanning herself with Amelia's stenographic pad. She's about as subtle as a crocodile stalking a water buffalo." She took the martini he was holding out to her. She sipped it and crossed her eyes. "Wow."

"Nice, eh, Minnie?"

"Very nice. And it's given me the courage to make my next move. And if Claire is watching me and faints, then you know I've struck pay dirt." She put her martini glass on the bar. "Guard this with your life." She crossed the room to the bookshelves on the opposite wall, the bookshelves that had been ransacked, and said loudly, "I know I saw one here."

Powell picked up the cue. "Saw one what?"

"A Bible."

Claire's head shot up. "What do you want with a Bible?"

"I'm looking for a quotation."

Villon asked Claire with concern, "What's wrong? What is it?"

Claire was hurrying to Myrna, who had taken the Bible from the shelf and opened it. Myrna gasped.

"Well, blow me down!" said Myrna triumphantly. "There's a false center been carved out of this Bible!"

"Give that to me!" shouted Claire, no longer faint, no longer Camille on the verge of slipping away from her Armand forever. Claire tried to snatch the Bible out of Myrna's hands but Myrna was too quick for her. She spun about in a pirouette of the sort that must have thrilled the audience at Grauman's Chinese when Myrna was dancing there. Mitchell Carewe made a move to assist Claire but Powell quickly crossed in front of him shouting, "What you got there, Minnie?"

"I think it's the little black book! It's not all that little and it's not all that black. In fact, it's just a plain old ordinary notebook with a spiral spine." She held the little book in her left hand while holding out the mutilated Bible to Jim Mallory, who quickly appropriated it. Myrna was heading back to the bar but Villon quickly intercepted her.

"I'll take the book, Myrna," said Villon.

"Oh dear. Now you've spoiled everything," said Myrna as she ceded the book to Villon. "I wanted to look for my husband's name."

"I suppose that dinky little thing is what all the fuss is about," said Powell blithely. "I'm terribly unimpressed." Freda snorted while Lucy Rockefeller, seemingly hypnotized by the object, seemed also unimpressed. Powell turned to Myrna. "But full marks to you, Minnie. That's what all that Bible business was about."

"Of course!" said Myrna, once again holding a martini and feeling very proud of herself. "Bibles are always laid out flat like defeated prizefighters, they're never stood on end."

Powell was proud of his Minnie. "Well, Herb Villon, have you no accolade to spare for our Miss Loy?"

"Sure. Good thinking, Myrna." Villon put the notebook in a jacket pocket, a snug fit.

Claire stood in front of him, hand outstretched, the color back in her cheeks. "I want that, Herb."

"I'll return it soon enough."

Hazel was waving the stenographic pad in their direction.

Myrna said to Powell, "Hazel's up to something."

Powell said, "I'd be surprised if she wasn't. Not very professional of Herb to let her appropriate the pad."

"I think it's an illustration of further method to his madness. I must say, he is one cool detective. Full marks to Herb. I admire him."

They heard Hazel ask, "What about Aunt Maidie?"

Claire spun about. "What about her?" She saw the stenographic pad moving back and forth. She also saw Mitchell Carewe closing in on Hazel.

So did Villon and Mallory. Villon ordered, "Stand back, Dr. Carewe."

Carewe was paralyzed by Villon's tone of voice. "Hazel, give it to Jim," said Villon.

"Sure," said Hazel. She handed the pad to Mallory, who pocketed it. Hazel's eyes never left Claire's face. "Is she really your aunt? You're sure she's not your mother?"

"She's really my aunt, you bitch," snapped Claire.

"What's the little boy's name?" asked Hazel.

"Leave him out of this." Claire was tense, her eyes were narrowed, her look sent a chill up Myrna's spine.

Powell had poured himself another martini and was feeling jauntier than ever. "Come, come, Claire. Where's your sense of sportsmanship? If the little boy is related to you, I should think you'd be proud of him. After all, bravely facing up to his affliction." He said to the others in the room, "The poor little tyke has been stricken with infantile paralysis. Polio."

Lucy Rockefeller looked on the verge of tears. "Oh, the poor kid. Polio. You mean like the lounge at the Beverly Hills Hotel?"

"That's the *Polo* lounge," said Myrna.

Claire said defiantly, "His name is Elmer. He's my son."

"I knew it!" cried Hazel.

Claire's hands were on her hips. "So what?"

"So a lot of things," said Bill Powell. "Such as why you need a lot of money. To take care of him. To see he's well provided for."

"And why not?" asked Myrna in defense of Claire and her monetary motive. "Haven't you heard of mother love? I must be the only actress in Hollywood who didn't discover in the final reel of a tear-jerker that the young attorney defending her on a charge of murder is really the child she gave up for adoption ten reels back."

"You're lucky to have escaped that fate, Minnie." Powell thought for a moment, "Have you ever given a child up for adoption?"

Myrna said softly, "Bill, I'd give the world for a child of my own." Powell nodded and raised his glass to her in a silent toast.

Villon shouted, "Hazel Dickson! You stay the hell off that phone! Louella Parsons can wait until I'm finished here!"

"But I'll miss the evening edition!" pleaded Hazel.

"Hazel dear," said Myrna, "there's always tomorrow, to repeat a maudlin cliché that I'm ashamed to have spoken."

Powell said, "Are we deliberately ignoring Amelia Hubbard?"

"I'm not," said Myrna. "I knew we'd get back to her in due time. It's now due time, am I right?"

"It is," said Villon. "Dr. Carewe, was Amelia Hubbard, by any chance, a patient of yours?"

Carewe said smoothly, "A long time ago I treated her for something, I forget what. But she wasn't a steady patient. I knew her through . . . er . . . Claire."

"Stands to reason," said Villon, reserving bringing up Audrey Manners, which he didn't think was called for at the moment. "Was she feeling ill today?"

Carewe shrugged. "How would I know?"

Villon showed him the page he had torn from Amelia's appointment book. "Do you recognize this?"

"Why yes. It's Claire's name. Penciled in for a ten A.M. appointment."

"I mean the phone number written at the bottom of the page. It's your office. I know because I dialed it and your receptionist identified it as such."

He looked at Claire then back to Villon. "Yes, she did call. I suppose there's nothing wrong in telling you why. She was concerned with the condition of Claire's health. I explained that that was privileged information and to be disclosed only at Claire's discretion.''

"I'm right in supposing she phoned after Claire left Amelia's apartment?''

"I don't know the exact time. But it was sometime after the noon hour.''

Villon said, "I don't think it was so much the condition of Claire's health that interested her.'' Carewe said nothing. Villon as he talked, was making his way slowly to the desk. Myrna was fascinated by the way he moved. It was almost sexily sinuous. Myrna was reminded of a reptile circling its prey as she had seen in a nature film not too long ago. "I think Amelia had money on her mind, much the way Claire, I think, still does.''

Claire said swiftly, "I promised Amelia a lot once I got my hands on money. She wouldn't have blackmailed . . .''

Villon was pleased with himself. The answers were coming easier then he thought they would. "Claire, we all have our Achilles' heel.''

Myrna said to Bill, "We sure do. I wonder what Hornblow is up to today.''

Villon was saying, "Amelia certainly had a very prominent one. Her near poverty-stricken existence. That apartment she lived in. It was the neatness that kept it from being exposed as a hovel. The cheap bottle of wine.''

"Manischewitz,'' contributed Hazel, "hardly vintage Dom Perignon.''

"And the clothes in her closet. I examined the closet after my associate'' — he indicated Jim Mallory — "found some important papers missing from the top shelf. I know they're important because when we were leaving for Hubbard's apartment, Claire chased after me to plead with me to find them and hold on to them before anyone else could see them. Unfortunately, Amelia's killer got to them first, thanks to Amelia.''

"What do you mean?'' asked Myrna.

"Amelia had gotten them off the shelf before her murderer arrived, to have them ready for him to read and see if Amelia was wrong in assessing their value. If they were valuable to Claire, they certainly had to be valuable to Amelia. And Amelia, poor desperate thing, needed something of value other than what she might have assumed were empty promises."

Myrna said to Powell, "He's almost as good as you are in your movies."

"Oh no he's not. He's left out a very important sentence: 'I suppose you're wondering why I've asked you all here.'"

Myrna smiled and sipped her martini.

Villon was opening the doctor's medical bag. Carewe seemed mesmerized. Villon widened the mouth of the bag, which was designed to give easily. He lit the desk lamp. The room had grown darker. It was almost twilight. Carewe had found his voice. "What are you doing there?"

Villon said, "I'm looking for evidence. That's my job. And look." He held up typewritten pages.

Claire cried out, "Herb! Please!"

"Claire darling," said Villon softly, although his voice made Hazel cringe, "I've got to nail me a killer. A very cruel, very brutal killer. A man who came to this house thinking he'd find you alone, Claire, and force the whereabouts of the little black book from you. Not because of what it contained about him, but because he needed it to swap for his gambling debts. Mobsters are terribly greedy, Claire. They're greedier than ex-wives. They saw the possibility of making a killing, no pun intended, with the little black book. Blackmail on a level higher than either Amelia or Claire could attain. There are more pages in the bag, these few I'm holding are but the tip of the iceberg." He placed them on the desk. He looked into the bag and saw the trophy he actually was hoping to find. He extracted a handkerchief from his rear pants pocket, reached into the doctor's bag, and brought forth an instrument with a sharp point that was covered with blood. He wrapped the handkerchief around the hilt to protect the fingerprints he was positive forensics would find there. "And here, I believe, is the tool that brought an end to Amelia Hubbard's life."

Myrna gasped. "Why, for crying out loud, I know what that is!"

Powell said, "Minnie, you never cease to amaze me. What the hell is it and how the hell do you know what it is? You know nothing about surgical tools."

"I most certainly do," said Myrna, eyes ablaze. "Two years or so back when Clark and I co-starred in *Men in White*. He was a physician and had to learn medical terminology and how to identify certain instruments and you know how hungry I get when there's a chance at gaining some knowledge, so I studied with Clark. He was grateful for my company because he's so dumb and knew I'd help him with the tough parts. Herb, that thing you're holding is called a xyster."

Powell asked, "As in 'How's your xyster'?"

"No, you facetious fool, as in did Amelia Hubbard know what hit her?"

"I don't think she did," said Herb Villon, who now held the sheet of paper he'd found in Amelia's typewriter. "After the murderer made his departure, she was able to type his name on this sheet of paper. Look, Dr. Carewe, here's your name and — don't be a goddamn fool, Doc, and put that automatic on the desk."

Claire said, "Mitchell, you heard him. Don't be a fool."

Carewe stared steadily at Villon, unaware that Zachary Forrest, who was out of Carewe's line of sight during Villon's demonstration, was slowly moving in on him with his revolver drawn.

Villon said to Carewe, "You're a bit reckless, Doctor. I had no proof you murdered Amelia and Fern Arnold. Oh, I could assume she phoned you with every intention of blackmailing you but what I had is circumstantial. Even with your name typed on the paper by Amelia, it could have been typed long before you murdered her. After all, you were on her mind. Your phone number was on a page of her appointment book."

Zachary Forrest pressed his gun into the small of Dr. Carewe's back. Carewe stiffened and slowly raised his hands. Forrest snatched the automatic away from Carewe.

Myrna said, "This is all terribly exciting, but Bill, haven't you guessed what Dr. Carewe was really after, what Amelia told him Claire had dictated to her?"

"Of course I've guessed, Miss Smarty Pants." He wished his mustache was twirlable because he had an urge to twirl it. "Dr. Carewe, I think what had you so frightened was Claire's revelation that back in 1932 you murdered Paul Bern."

Villon shouted, "Hazel! Stay away from that phone!"

NINETEEN

*H*azel was in a rage. Her hand was just a few inches from the phone, a few inches from dialing Louella Parsons, a few inches from earning a few hundred dollars for a scoop that would land Louella's column on the front page. Paul Bern's murderer unmasked at last! It didn't occur to her that not that many people would remember Paul Bern's murder. In Los Angeles, yes, in the rest of the country, the rest of the world, no. Myrna stared at Powell. He was looking at Paul Bern's murderer. He was facing the prospect of an old scandal involving his beloved paramour, Jean Harlow, making headlines again. What would it do to her? What would the effect be on Louis B. Mayer and Howard Strickling?

All hell broke loose.

Freda shrieked as Dr. Carewe spun around and wrestled Zachary Forrest for his revolver. His powerful right connected with Forrest's chin and sent him reeling backward. Mallory pulled his revolver and shouted at Carewe, who had retrieved his automatic from the desk top.

Villon shouted at Mallory, "Don't kill the bastard! Just wing him!"

Carewe was crazed. His world had come crashing down around his ears. He fired several wild shots. Myrna and Powell ducked behind the bar, each holding a martini and not spilling a drop. Freda and Lucy had taken shelter behind the couch, while Villon, revolver drawn, shoved Lazlo to one side. Lazlo shouted an epithet in Hungarian. Forrest got back to his feet and together with Mallory, wrestled Carewe to the floor. Mallory brought his gun handle down on the doctor's wrist. The automatic fell onto the floor while the doctor cried out in pain.

Powell and Myrna slowly emerged from behind the bar. "Ah!" said Powell, watching Mallory handcuff Carewe, "the good doctor's been subdued."

"You mean bad doctor," said Myrna while Carewe continued to moan in pain. "Oh good. He's hurt."

Powell said, " 'Physician, heal thyself,' " but Carewe didn't hear him.

The commotion gave Hazel the opportunity to phone Louella Parsons. Louella excitedly had Dorothy, her assistant, phone the city desk to stop the presses. As Louella herself frequently said, "Tell them I've got a scee-oop!"

Mallory and Forrest pulled Carewe to his feet. His eyes met Myrna's. She said to him, "Little man, you've had a busy day."

Villon was looking around the room for Claire. Had she run out? Freda and Lucy were surfacing from behind the couch. "Where's Claire?" he shouted.

"Here!" cried Lazlo. "Here!"

Claire lay on her back in front of the fireplace, the very spot where Villon and the others had found the body of Fern Arnold earlier in the day. Villon knelt at Claire's side, calling her name.

"Dear God!" said Myrna, "she can't be dead. The little boy needs her."

Villon shouted to Mallory, "Get an ambulance!" The room had filled with detectives alerted by the gunfire and one hurried out to his car to call for an ambulance over his radio.

Hazel was telling Louella that Claire Young had been shot, perhaps fatally.

"How marvelous!" yelped Louella, "another scee–oop!"

Villon cradled Claire in his arms. He had felt for her pulse. She was still alive but bleeding profusely from a stomach wound.

Carewe shouted, "For Christ's sake let me help her!"

Villon said to Mallory and Forrest. "Bring him here. One of you bring his kit."

Myrna said to Powell, "Claire needs help, but I wouldn't trust Carewe. Would you — Bill? What's wrong? He hasn't shot you too!"

"No, no, Minnie, I'm perfectly fine," he said.

"Like hell you are. You're pale as a ghost."

"That's what ghosts do to me."

"What ghosts?" Myrna was slightly bewildered.

"Actually, public ghost number one. Paul Bern."

The detective who had radioed for an ambulance returned to say it was on its way. He also said the press was getting out of hand. What were the gun shots? Who's been hurt? Who's dead? Villon waved him away. Carewe had been freed and was kneeling at Claire's side, Mallory and Forrest standing over him with guns drawn.

Hazel, at the phone, one hand covering the mouthpiece, yelled to Villon, "She still alive?" Villon shot her a filthy look. Hazel realized Claire was being treated by Carewe. Her eyes widened with delight. She spoke into the phone, "Louella! How's this for cockeyed human interest! The cops are letting Carewe treat Claire Young. She got hit by one of his wild shots!" She was mad with unrestrained joy. "Is this a story or is this a story! It's absolutely exclusive! I don't think even that gang of vultures outside know what's been going on!" She yelled to the detective who had radioed for the ambulance, "Do those vultures outside know what's going on?" He reassured her they didn't, but it couldn't be held from them too much longer — in the distance could be heard the siren of the approaching ambulance. Its sound could send the press into a feeding frenzy. Hazel told Louella the story was exclusively hers.

Myrna had been doing her best to assuage Powell. Jean Harlow was one of the press's favorite actresses. She was always cooperative, rarely refused an interview, posed tirelessly for their cameras, and in their words was a "good Joe." Myrna was sure they'd treat her kindly. Powell hoped she was right. The Hollywood press, especially the international members, were a vicious lot. Powell was sure they ate their young and now tried to eat each other.

Carewe had cut away a portion of Claire's dress to expose her wound. He had staunched the bleeding and dressed the wound as best he could while advising Villon she needed to be in a hospital as soon as possible.

Hazel was on her toes for a better look at the wounded madam. She said to Louella, "Looks like she's still out of it. She doesn't look too good to me." The ambulance had arrived and the attendants had hurried in with a stretcher. One attendant said in shock, "Oh my God! It's Claire!"

Freda cried out in recognition, "My sweetheart! It's me! Your Freda!"

The attendant blushed and said in a dull voice, "Hullo, Freda," and then helped strap Claire to the stretcher. Mallory had placed the cuffs back on Carewe's wrists.

Hazel yelled to Myrna, "Has she become conscious yet?"

"No, dear," said Myrna. "We haven't heard her say, 'Where am I?'" She now disapproved of Hazel and at the earliest opportunity planned to tell her so. The callous bitch. Myrna's arm was around Powell's shoulders and he patted her hand in gratitude. His Irish mother had told him a long time ago there was nothing as comforting as the warmth of a solid friendship, and Myrna was indeed a solid friend. The solid friend now voiced the need for a fresh martini. Powell's hands flew to work. Where mixing a drink was concerned, he was like a mailman: "Neither snow nor sleet, etc. etc. etc." As he deftly concocted the brew, he said to Myrna, who was watching Claire being carried out with an honor guard of detectives surrounding her to protect her from the press, "I suppose this will sound rather cruel . . ."

"Go right ahead, Bill," said Myrna. "I've been a witness to a lot of cruelty today. Especially woman's inhumanity to woman."

"I was thinking of Claire and her desperate need for money. Well, if she dies, there'll be no double indemnity clause to worry Aunt Maidie."

Freda was saying to Lucy, "We must go with Claire. We can't let her be by herself now. Lazlo! We're going to the hospital. Bring your fiddle."

"Of course I bring my fiddle! I shall serenade Claire back to consciousness with a medley of Irving Berlin." He hurried after Freda and Lucy, planning to begin with "Russian Lullaby" and "Alexander's Ragtime Band."

Mallory and Zachary Forrest were hustling Carewe out of the room to a squad car and thence to the precinct, where he would be booked for the murders of Fern Arnold and Amelia Hubbard. Then later, if Claire didn't pull through, for the added murder of Claire Young. And since there was no statute of limitation for murder, he also would have to answer for the murder of Paul Bern.

Hazel was finally off the phone and at the bar toasting herself for beating the competition. Myrna watched as Hazel's face flushed with excitement and self-approval, and said to Powell, "I disapprove of her thoroughly, but I have to admit, she's one hell of a news hen. But she'd better not expect a Christmas card from me."

They heard the sound of the ambulance siren as it sped away, followed by the revving of auto engines and the skidding of wheels as the press pursued the ambulance.

Hazel downed her drink and responded to the angry look on Villon's face. "Don't stay too mad too long or I won't let you in on a big secret in Amelia's steno pad."

Villon said angrily, "There are others who can read shorthand."

"That's right. But I wouldn't be too quick to get it into the hands of just anyone."

Myrna interrupted, still concerned with Claire Young and her son. "Herb, now what happens to the notebook, the steno pad, the papers Dr. Carewe stole?"

"They eventually get turned over to Claire's lawyer. If she doesn't pull through, I assume the kid and the aunt are her legal heirs. Claire's lawyer is smart, and surprisingly enough, very honest. I know Derwitt. I've used him myself in the past."

Myrna couldn't resist. "Recommended by Audrey Manners?"

Villon took her remark good-naturedly. "Audrey was one hell of a gal. Claire Young is another story. Stop drinking so much, Hazel, it's too early to get tanked."

"It's never too early to get tanked," said Powell as he refreshed his and Myrna's drinks. "Herb, can I interest you?"

Sinking into a chair, Herb said, "As a matter of fact, yes, screw regulations."

Hazel said, "It's after sundown," as she went about the room turning on lamps, "you're off duty."

"I'm not off duty until I check with the precinct."

Powell said, as he poured drinks and then distributed them, "Am I wrong in deducing that it was Carewe as an angry young intern who killed Bern? Odd to kill a man for refusing you a loan."

"He killed him because he was jealous of his relationship with Audrey."

Myrna's eyebrows were raised. "Are you saying Bern's marriage to Baby was a marriage of convenience? He didn't love her?"

Powell spoke up. "Minnie, Paul Bern was a very odd character."

Myrna said, "I've got a feeling that's an understatement."

Powell said, "Baby told me as much about him as she could ever fathom. They never had sex."

"No!" cried Myrna.

Hazel and Villon sat quietly. Hazel had poured herself a fresh brandy and Villon was savoring his drink.

Powell continued, "He loved women in his own immature way. Actually, it wasn't love as we like to think we experience love, it was adulation. In Bern's eyes, women belonged on a pedestal. Barbara Lamarr. Jean Harlow. They were goddesses. You worship at the shrine of a goddess, but you don't have sex with her."

Myrna couldn't believe what she was hearing. "Are you insinuating he was a homosexual?"

"He wasn't anything," said Powell. "He was that sort of tiresome creature known as a studio executive. He needed the company of beautiful women to create and sustain the myth that he was a boudoir Lothario. He was no such thing. But he was courtly and a gentleman and very knowledgeable. He had a fine mind and liked to share his knowledge with these women, and they, in turn, welcomed his kind of attention. It was uncomplicated. Paul was a witty man. Baby told me it was a relief to meet someone like him. He made no demands. He just wanted the added celebrity of being her husband. Audrey Manners had been one of his girls. He set her up in business. Carewe was nuts about Audrey and is still nuts about Claire, or so I assume."

"Nuts enough to tell her she was dying?" Myrna was enchanting when she looked incredulous.

"I assume she's genuinely dying. He wouldn't lie to her, would he?"

Myrna said wisely. "I think he's lied to her and if she survives, I suggest she get a few more reliable opinions. And as for still being in love with her, why come here to kill her and search for the little black book?"

Villon said, "Maybe he came here to kill Fern Arnold." He had their undivided attention. "You saw them together last night at Griselda's Cave. I think they were having an affair and Claire wasn't wise to it. I think Carewe was romancing Fern to get to the little black book and use it to get the mob off his back. Remember, his solid reputation and his solid practice were also at stake. I think at Griselda's Fern was finally wise to the fact that she was being used. She didn't like that. She liked getting laid, but she didn't like being used. And also there was the likelihood she was first in line to get this whole kit and kaboodle from Claire." He waved an arm to encompass the room. "Carewe also knew Claire was dictating her memoirs to Amelia Hubbard because Fern told him so."

"Do you know this for sure?" asked Powell.

"You got a better supposition?"

"I'd like to pin this on Louis B. Mayer. Any chance?" asked Powell.

Villon laughed. "Not a hope in hell."

Myrna asked, "Why did Amelia phone Carewe?"

"Probably because he'd made her an offer for the pages and she said she'd think it over and let him know. She was letting him know. I think she turned him down, much as she needed the money, because she still had some decency left and decided not to double-cross Claire. She probably said as much to Carewe who, by now, was desperate. First he kills Fern, then he gets Amelia, and he was probably planning to come back here and finish off Claire. He didn't count on me deciding to come and see Claire with Jim and that one," pointing at Hazel, "in tow."

Hazel's eyes were narrowed into slits as Myrna said, "I'm so glad Amelia Hubbard decided to remain faithful to Claire. There are so few women in this life" — she shot a quick look at Hazel, who was too busy staring daggers at Villon — "who are true blue and can be trusted. Herb, if Amelia has no family, I'd like to pay for her funeral."

Powell said, "Minnie, you're an angel. I'll split the cost with you."

"Now, you're sure about that?" asked Myrna. "It means buying a plot in a cemetery and a headstone and something very nice for her to be buried in. Maybe I'll talk to Adrian at Metro about designing a lovely dress for her." She was feeling very good about herself and wondered if there was any chance of Louis B. Mayer seeing his way clear to letting her play Joan of Arc with perhaps Mickey Rooney as the Dauphin.

Villon said to Hazel, "It'll do you no good to keep giving me that dirty look. You shouldn't be very proud of your behavior, gassing with that alcoholic windbag Parsons while Claire lay dying."

Hazel said forthrightly, "That gassing is how I earn my living. You think I enjoy behaving like a cobra in heat? I don't know any other way to make a fast buck or buck a slow fast and I'd never make it as a prostitute."

Myrna reserved comment. She was woman enough to know that dirty look or no dirty look, Hazel Dickson was very much in love with Herb Villon and she didn't doubt for one minute that he was equally in love with her.

Villon said, "I'm tired and I'm hungry. Who's for Griselda's? I need a steak and french fries."

"My treat," said Powell magnanimously. "Minnie?" She was off in a world of her own. "Minnie? Where are you?"

"At Amelia's funeral. I'm going to get Jeanette and Nelson to sing the "Indian Love Call" and perhaps Jimmy Durante to tell a few jokes because funerals are much too somber. Did I hear someone suggest Griselda's? Oh good. I'm famished."

Hazel was standing with Villon and fixing his tie, which had gone askew. "I think you ought to take time tomorrow to go out to Venice and visit little Elmer and Aunt Maidie."

Villon said, "Now you're reading my mind."

"Oh good," said Hazel, "because it's in Amelia's stenographic pad."

Villon was bemused. "What is?"

"Claire identifies Elmer's father." Powell and Loy were now in Hazel's thrall. Hazel pinched Villon's cheek. She said sweetly, "Hello, Daddy."

Myrna said to Villon, "Congratulations, Herb. Bill, do you think it's much too late to throw Herb a baby shower?"

(